VEIL

JENNA ST. JAMES

Cheryl,

Enjoy!

Jenna!

Veiled in Murder

JENNA ST. JAMES BOOKS

Ryli Sinclair Mystery Series Order

Picture Perfect Murder
Girls' Night Out Murder
Old-Fashioned Murder
Bed, Breakfast, and Murder
Veiled in Murder
Bachelorettes and Bodies
Rings, Veils, and Murder
Last Stop Murder

Sullivan Sisters Mystery Series Order

Murder on the Vine
Burning Hot Murder
Prepear to Die

DEDICATION

To Maddy...thanks for always wanting to play the part of Aunt Shirley when I do my final read.

CHAPTER 1

"I still can't believe we got an appointment so fast," Mom said as we walked through the front door of Quilter's Paradise.

"This would be a great store," Aunt Shirley said, "if I gave two hoots about quilting or sewing. But the colors are cool. Matches my hair." She pushed up one side of her pastel purple, blue, and green hair with her hand.

Quilter's Paradise recently opened its doors in Granville, Missouri. Their first store, located in Columbia, was a huge success, so they decided to expand. The fact the owners chose Granville for their second store was a big deal. I think it's because not only is Granville centrally located between Brywood and Kansas City, but there's also a large Amish population in the next county over. Whatever the reason, Granville was happy for the revenue. By the number of cars in the parking lot, the business seemed to be doing well.

"I spoke with a lady by the name of Samantha Kingston," I said. "She told me to go to the back of the store and tell the person behind the counter that I was her eleven o'clock appointment."

Today I was ordering my wedding veil. Yes, you heard right…my wedding veil. Garrett Kimble, ex-military hottie and current Granville Police Chief, asked me to marry him after my near-death experience in April.

To be fair, it was probably my fourth or fifth brush with death—after that many times, you lose count. But it was enough of a push for him to realize he loved me, our ten-year age difference didn't matter, and he wanted to marry me and have babies with me.

More like I think he's hoping if he marries me he can keep better track of me. But I'll take it…and him.

4

Paige, my currently-pregnant best friend who married my brother five months ago, put her hand in mine as we strolled down the aisle toward the back of the store. "I'm happy you decided on doing the veil."

I wasn't so sure about the veil. But I could tell it meant a lot to Mom, so I agreed. Garrett and I decided we'd get married during my favorite month—October. Only four more months, and I'd no longer be Ryli Sinclair but Ryli Kimble.

A very sobering thought.

I already have my wedding dress, flowers, and venue picked out. We're getting married in Mom's backyard. I decided on a backyard wedding because I still break out in a cold sweat when I think about Paige and Matt's wedding. That was another one of those near-death experiences for me.

Two ladies were behind a long counter in the back of the store. Even though their backs were to us and they were whispering, body posture told me they were both upset.

"Hello?" Mom said as we approached the counter.

The two ladies quickly turned around and plastered fake smiles on their faces. The older woman took the lead. "Hello, and welcome to Quilter's Paradise. My name is Blair Watkins, owner of Quilter's Paradise. And this is Samantha Kingston. Are you the eleven o'clock appointment?"

"Yes, ma'am," Mom answered.

I let Mom take charge so I could study the two women in front of me. Eight months ago, I would have never thought to assess someone I first meet and size them up threat-wise. But too many close calls have made it necessary that I now be on the offensive instead of defensive. Just one of the many lessons I've learned in the self-defense class Aunt Shirley and I take through the Manor. We've only had one session so far, but the lesson has made an impact. Our next class was tomorrow night and was taught by my boss and retired Marine, Hank Perkins.

My first impression of Blair Watkins was that she was highly stressed and agitated. It used to be when I met someone I would take in their physical appearance, but now I look at their body language. Her pinched mouth coupled with furrowed brows let me know she was about to throw down on someone.

Samantha Kingston on the other hand looked like she was about to burst into tears. She was blinking rapidly and her face was red and drawn tight.

"We are so happy to have you ladies with us today," Blair said. "And on such a happy occasion. Who is the lucky bride?"

I almost didn't raise my hand. It was a dumb question to ask as far as I was concerned. I mean, you had Paige, sporting a huge wedding ring on her finger and obviously pregnant. Aunt Shirley, who played Kick-the-Can with Jesus when he was a boy. Mom—well, okay, it could have been Mom. And me. I mean, why wouldn't I be the obvious choice here on who the bride was?

"Congratulations," Blair said when I finally raised my hand. "Come on back to our privacy rooms and Samantha will get started on your measurements for the veil."

There were three partitioned-off rooms, and Blair took us to the middle room. It was the size of a standard bedroom, with two loveseats pushed against one wall and a desk on the opposite wall. There was a small platform sitting in front of a full-length tri-fold mirror, and more ribbons, tulle, push pins, measuring tapes, and other sewing paraphernalia than I'd ever seen in my life. I felt a trickle of sweat roll down the back of my neck.

"Ladies, make yourselves comfortable on the sofas," Blair said. "Can I get you something to drink?"

"Bottled waters would be great," Mom said quickly. She must have seen Aunt Shirley open her mouth like I had. Aunt Shirley would take the offer of a drink as an invitation for booze of some sort.

Blair left the room, leaving us alone with Samantha. She still looked shaken, but she was doing her best to breathe through her discomfort.

"Ryli, can I get you to stand on the platform, please?" Samantha softly requested.

I set my purse down on the floor by one of the sofas and stepped up on the platform. I felt like I was on display. Not a comfortable feeling for me.

"You have your dress picked out, yes?" Samantha asked.

I nodded. "I bought it a few weeks ago. I pretty much already knew what I wanted."

"Good. Tell me about it. Does it have a long train? Is it short? Give me an idea of the dress so we can talk about the length of the veil."

The wedding dress itself was simple yet elegant. "It's a floor-length ball gown with a lace bodice and off-the-shoulder cap sleeves. It has a sweetheart neckline, a cinched waist, and the bottom is completely made of tulle." I loved the fact it was so fluffy and big, yet stopped just short of touching the ground. I didn't want to worry the whole night about getting the dress dirty.

Even though we were getting married outside in October, I went with the shorter sleeves. Mom had already assured me that if for some reason it was unnaturally cool that day, she had two outdoor heaters she could turn on, and we could borrow more if we needed. Usually October in Missouri was a crapshoot as far as weather went.

"Sounds lovely," Samantha said. "What about headpiece? Do you have an idea in mind of what you want?"

I turned and looked at myself in the mirror. I conjured up the dress and thought about my hair and how I wanted it to look on that day. "I'm thinking of wearing my hair down, yet partially up." I took my hair out of the ponytail it was in, shook it out, then gathered a little of the hair back, leaving hair to frame my face. "I don't want anything big on top of my head, hiding my face. Can we maybe start the veil in the back where the hair will be gathered?"

"I think that would be perfect." Samantha turned me sideways in the mirror so I could see the back of my hair. "Something that is basically an extension of the gathered hair. Coming a little bit up and off, maybe down to here?" She brought the measuring tape down a little past my rear.

I caught Mom's eye. "I think so. What do you think?"

Mom blinked back tears before answering. "I think that will look beautiful. I'm glad you decided on the veil."

I chuckled inside. What she means is she's glad I listened to *her* and decided on the veil. "I think that will be perfect then, Samantha."

Blair strode into the room carrying four bottled waters. She handed them to each of us then turned to Samantha. "Can I see you out in the hall for a moment, please."

Samantha stiffened but smiled. "Sure."

Samantha walked over to the desk and handed me a book. "Why don't you look over some styles real quick and let me know what you like. Also, if you'd like you can sign up for the weekly newsletter so you can know what's on sale for the weekend. We can either send you a store email or a store text on your phone. You can get newsletters, coupons, all sorts of things."

The two ladies walked silently out of the room and shut the door behind them. Mom, Aunt Shirley, and Paige walked over to look at the book with me. A few seconds later we heard arguing.

"So you're telling me you have no idea how this is happening?" Blair hissed.

"I honestly don't," Samantha said. I could hear the tears in her voice. "I don't understand what's going on."

Blair huffed angrily. "Me, either. I also just got off the phone with Lexi, and she said three more one-star reviews have come in over the last twenty-four hours. As the manager, I hold you personally responsible."

I looked at Aunt Shirley and made a pained face. She lifted her eyebrows but said nothing. The walls were way too thin to be airing dirty laundry.

"I understand," Samantha said. "I just don't understand—"

"I know," Blair said snidely. "You just don't understand how this is happening. So you've said again and again." There was a brief pause and I thought maybe they were done, but then Blair continued. "I'm telling you right now, if you don't get this resolved quickly, you will be fired. Do you understand?"

I heard Samantha gasp. "Yes, ma'am. I understand."

"Good," Blair said.

A few seconds later a red-faced Samantha opened the door and quietly shut it behind her. We all tried to pretend we hadn't heard anything, but it was no use. She walked over to where we were and I put my hand on her arm.

"Are you okay?" I asked.

Samantha closed her eyes briefly then plastered on a fake smile. "No. I'm sorry you overheard that. Here it is supposed to be a happy day for you and you probably can't enjoy it with all this yelling."

"You don't have to pretend for us," Paige said. "It's okay to cry."

That was Samantha's undoing. She put her head in her hands and started sobbing. Paige panicked and looked at me, shrugged her shoulders, and mouthed she was sorry.

I went over to the desk and brought back a box of tissue. "Here. Take some tissue." I looked at Aunt Shirley as Samantha blew her nose.

"Why don't you tell us what's going on," Aunt Shirley commanded.

I heard a small groan from Mom.

"Oh, it's nothing, really." Samantha rubbed her hands together. "So, did you find a veil you liked?"

I actually had. "I'll show it to you on one condition. You tell me what's going on."

Samantha worked her lower lip between her teeth. I could tell she didn't want to involve us. But the sale must have won out because she nodded her head.

"Have a seat and I'll tell you what's been going on." Samantha waited until we were all situated on the couch before she began. "We've only been open for about six months now. And at first things were going great. Blair brought Lexi, the social media manager, and me over from the Columbia store. And like I said, things were going well. Then about two months ago we started noticing things."

"What kind of things?" Aunt Shirley asked.

"Well, we always send out our email flyers for the upcoming weekend sale on Thursday evening. Yet somehow a major competitor in Kansas City would have the exact same thing on sale."

"I just signed us all up for the weekly newsletters." I crinkled my nose. "I have to say, that sounds a little more than coincidental."

"I know. Plus, we are suddenly getting bombarded with bad reviews. Lexi is losing her mind over all these things."

"What does this Lexi person think is happening?" Mom asked.

I knew she'd get drawn in even though she didn't want to.

Samantha shrugged. "Lexi and I have been with the company since the very beginning, when it was just a small shop in Columbia. We were actually Blair's first hires. I think Lexi believes someone is intentionally sabotaging the company."

"What about the reviews?" I asked. "Are they legitimate?"

Samantha chewed on her bottom lip. "It seems so. I mean they drop just the right amount of hints that we know they were actually in the store. Maybe they'll describe what one of us was wearing or what we were doing at the time of the complaint. So, yeah, I guess they are legit. And what's worse, according to Daniel Watkins—he's not only Blair's husband, but the accountant who does books for both stores—the store here in Granville is losing money. Big time losing money. We're down to only six workers, and that's including Blair and her husband."

This place is packed with customers. How can they be losing money suddenly?

"I wonder why Blair is totally blaming you," Aunt Shirley said.

Samantha's eyes filled up with tears again. "I'm not exactly sure. I have some theories. But the end result is this—if things don't improve soon, we may have to close shop."

CHAPTER 2

"I feel sorry for that girl," Aunt Shirley said as she situated herself in the front seat of the Falcon.

I carefully pulled out of the parking lot and headed back to town. The Falcon was Aunt Shirley's pride and joy. A 1965 turquoise Ford Falcon with purple ghost flames on the sides, and under the hood was a stock 302 with an Edelbrock fuel injection. The barely-there dashboard was done in the same turquoise color, and the bucket seats in the front and bench seat in the back were pristine white with turquoise stitching.

And now the Falcon is *my* pride and joy. Aunt Shirley lost her driving privileges about the same time she got put into Oak Grove Manor. Let's just say after some pretty sketchy antics, Mom and Garrett decided Aunt Shirley needed to have a permanent room at the Manor. The good thing about the Manor is that it's an assisted living facility, not really a nursing home. Aunt Shirley can come and go as she pleases and she still gets her own apartment.

"Do you want me to stop so we can grab some lunch?" I asked.

Mom shook her head. "I'm not really all that hungry right now. But you girls feel free to drop me off at the house and go back out."

"Actually," Paige piped up from the backseat next to Mom, "I need to go home and get some work finished, too."

I caught her eye in the rearview mirror. I knew that was a lie. She gave me a wink.

"Looks like it's just you and me, Ryli," Aunt Shirley said gleefully. Aunt Shirley would do anything to get out of going back to the Manor.

I dropped Mom and Paige off at Mom's house. Paige and Matt live about five doors down from my mom, so Paige could walk home when she wanted to. I sent Paige a silent look reminding her I'd be by her house around one so we could go run our errand.

"I say Steve's Sub Shop for lunch," Aunt Shirley said as I backed the Falcon out of Mom's driveway.

"Subs it is."

Usually Aunt Shirley and I would just run through the Burger Barn's drive-thru, but recently Aunt Shirley has been getting more serious about the two of us getting into shape. I knew deep down it was because she still wasn't completely over how close I came to getting shot back in April. Luckily the bullet just grazed my arm...but it took a toll on Aunt Shirley's mental health.

Steve's Sub Shop was packed, so we made our way to the back of the line and waited. We were next in line when I noticed someone glaring at me. I suppressed a groan. It was Willa Trindle.

Not only did Willa and I go to high school together, but we also attend the same church. She's a lot like her momma—gossipy and mean-spirited. We've pretty much always had a hate-hate relationship that goes back as far as high school. She never had a desire to go out for cheerleading until I did. She made it, I didn't. When I sang at the school talent show my senior year, she decided to sing *and* dance. When Willa found out I was going to audition for a part in the school play, she tried out for the same role. She would sit across from me in Sunday school class and kick me under the table and then try and say it was an accident.

I hoped my fake smile and half-hearted wave would suffice as I slid down the counter and told the guy working which veggies I wanted on my sandwich.

I paid for our sandwiches and Aunt Shirley grabbed them and headed for the door. I walked out of the shop and was glad to see Willa wasn't still hovering by the door.

"Yoohoo. Ryli, is that you?"

I spoke too soon. Standing next to the Falcon was Willa Trindle. But then I blinked in surprise because standing next to Willa was Samantha Kingston. And then it clicked. I'd forgotten Willa worked at Quilter's Paradise.

I could hear Aunt Shirley grumble beside me, but I ignored her and put on a smile. "Hey, Willa. Hi, Samantha. Out for lunch?"

"Yes," Willa gushed. "You know Samantha Kingston, I assume. I heard you were at the quilt shop today." Willa gave me a syrupy-sweet smile. "I'm so excited for your wedding to Garrett. I can't wait to see you on your wedding day!"

Aaannnd….there it was. The subtle we-aren't-really-friends-but-I-better-be-invited-to-your-wedding threat. I didn't want her at my wedding, but I knew there was probably no way of getting around that. After all, we attend the same church.

I made a non-committal noise and took a harder look at Samantha. She still looked pale and upset. "How're you doing, Samantha?"

Samantha gave me a forced smile. "Good. It's so nice to run into you again, but we better head back." She looked like she wanted to say something more.

Aunt Shirley must have also picked up on it. "Willa, where did you girls park?"

Willa pointed across the street.

"Well, why don't I walk you to your car and you can tell me how your momma is doing. I didn't get a chance to speak with her Sunday at church."

Willa's face lit up and she looped her arm around Aunt Shirley's. I almost laughed at the angst on Aunt Shirley's face. "Momma is doing great. She had to go to the doctor last week because her gout is acting up. But otherwise…"

Their voices trailed off and I was left alone with Samantha.

"Ryli, I've been thinking about what you said to me. About why this might be happening at the store. And I think I have a couple theories. I don't have time to go into them right now because I really do need to get back to the store. Do you think you could come by tomorrow morning before the store opens and we could talk?"

I wasn't expecting this, but I did want to help her out. "Sure. What time?"

Samantha let out a rush of breath and gave a shaky laugh. "How about tomorrow morning around seven. The store opens at eight, so that gives us plenty of time to talk before the other workers start to come in. I'll leave the back door open for you. I'll be in the back where we were today working on a couple orders."

"Can I bring Aunt Shirley? She used to be a private investigator, so she might have ideas on how to help. Just don't tell her I said that."

Samantha laughed at my attempt at humor. "Sure. I look forward to seeing you both tomorrow morning around seven."

She crossed the street and walked over to where Willa and Aunt Shirley were still in deep conversation. Well, Willa was still in conversation, Aunt Shirley looked like she wanted to brain Willa. Samantha said something and Willa got in the car and they drove away.

"My God, that girl can prattle on about nothing," Aunt Shirley said as she got in the Falcon. "Like I give two figs about her momma's gout. Yuck! Did you get anything good?"

I smiled. "Thanks for taking the hint and taking one for the team. Samantha wants us to swing by the store tomorrow before they open. Around seven. She wants to talk with us about a couple theories she has about what's going on."

"Sounds good. Now, let's get back to the office. I'm starving."

My stomach sank. I was afraid of this. "Actually, I told Hank I needed the rest of the day off. I have something I need to do this afternoon."

"Like what?"

I sighed. When you were constantly surrounded by family, it was sometimes impossible to have a life outside of them. "Like something I need to do. It's private."

"Are you doing something naughty and kinky for Garrett?" Aunt Shirley asked. "Like piercing a body part, or maybe buying some—"

"No!" I cut her off. I didn't want to know where she was going with that thought. "It's nothing like that. I just need some alone time for a bit."

Aunt Shirley frowned and then stuck out her bottom lip. "Fine. I understand. It's no big deal. I have plenty of stuff to do at my apartment to keep me busy. Maybe I'll go make friends with the people across the hall. Maybe they'll invite me in and kill me. But you go on and go about your secret life. I'm sure I'll be fine."

I wasn't having any of it. "I'm sure you will be."

Aunt Shirley scowled at me but didn't say anything else as I pulled into the Manor. She stuck her sandwich bag into her purse and shot out of the Falcon. I could tell she was put out.

"Tell Old Man Jenkins I said hi," I said, trying to unhurt her feelings. "And I'll be by around seven tomorrow morning to pick you up. I'll text when I'm heading over."

"I'd say have a good day, but for all I know you're going into Brywood to knock over a convenience store."

"That was fast," Paige said as I walked in her front door a few minutes later.

"I still need to eat my sandwich then I'll be ready."

We made small talk as I ate, but I could tell Paige was distracted. She was constantly rubbing her already-huge belly. I admit I don't know a whole lot about babies, but it seemed to me she was pretty big for only being a week or two along in her second trimester.

I finished eating and Paige offered to drive. That was fine by me. While I love the Falcon, I knew Paige preferred a more pampered ride. And her Tahoe was definitely a pampered ride.

Thirty minutes later we pulled into a parking lot and Paige shut off her car. "Thank you for coming in with me today. I know this is probably something I should be doing with Matt, but I think I have an idea of what's going on. And if I'm right, I want it to be a surprise."

"Like a good surprise, right?" Because for the life of me I couldn't think of why she would want me to go to her first ultrasound instead of Matt. When she invited me last week and demanded I keep it a secret, I was scared to death. I thought maybe something was wrong with the baby.

We walked into the doctor's office and I took a seat in one of the chairs while Paige went to check in. She came back over, sat next to me, then started chugging a bottled water.

"I have to have a full bladder," Paige said when she noticed my strange look.

"Oh." I felt stupid and awkward. I knew this was probably something I was going to have to do shortly. Garrett was ten years older than me. He would be forty next year, and he told me he was ready to start a family whenever I was. I personally thought he was going about it all wrong. If he was going to wait on me to be ready, he was going to be waiting a long time.

Twenty minutes later the nurse called Paige and me back to the room. We walked down the narrow corridor and into one of the empty rooms with the promise that the technician would be in shortly.

"My heart is beating wildly in my chest," I admitted as Paige wiggled up onto the table.

She laughed. "I think that's supposed to be my line." She squirmed on the table. "I hope she hurries because I really have to pee."

The sonogram angels were smiling down on Paige, because a few minutes later the technician came in. "How're we feeling today?"

"Anxious, excited, nervous, scared," I said.

Paige giggled as the technician gave me a quizzical look. I was aware she was talking to Paige, but I couldn't help myself.

"I'm so glad I brought you," Paige said. I stood up and held her hand, excited beyond words that I'd be one of the first people to see the baby.

The technician tucked a white paper cloth inside Paige's waistband and then lifted her shirt up. "I'm going to put the jelly on now."

I watched in amazement as the technician smeared a clear-like substance over Paige's protruding belly then took a wand-like contraption and placed it on Paige's stomach.

"Oh, I felt him kick!" Paige exclaimed.

I looked around the small room when I heard a fast *whoosh, whoosh* sound fill the air.

"Heartbeat," the technician said as she smiled at me. "Right here you can see the skull and the body."

Paige sucked in her breath as we watched the baby's body emerge before us as the technician pointed out certain body parts.

A thousand emotions flooded me at the sight of my niece or nephew on the screen. I tried to think of something to say to Paige, but words failed me. Sad to think I make my living writing, and yet I had no words to express what I was feeling at that exact moment.

"Now let's look and see if your suspicion is correct," the technician said.

I glanced down at Paige. Tears fell from her eyes as she watched the baby on the screen. If I was feeling this way, she had to be triple the emotion. I didn't know how she could stand it.

The technician moved the wand around a little more. "It's just as you thought."

Paige sucked in a breath and my heart dropped. Was there something wrong? I sandwiched Paige's hand in mine, prepared for the worst.

"So let me show you this. Here's the first heartbeat." The loud, rhythmic *whoosh, whoosh* of the baby's heart filled the room again. "And here's the second."

Wait...what?

And then it hit me. "Omigod! Omigod! You're having *twins?*" I bounced up and down in excitement. "Twins! Is this why you wanted me to go? Omigosh. I thought maybe something was wrong and that's why you wanted me here."

Paige shook her head. "Nope. I wanted you here because this is exactly what I thought was going on. There were just too many signs. And with it falling on Father's Day weekend, I wanted to really surprise Matt."

"Oh," I laughed. "Believe me, he will be *more* than surprised. We're gonna have to pick him up off the floor. Oh, I can't wait! How're you gonna tell him?"

"I've been tossing things around ever since I suspected," Paige said mysteriously.

"Are we finding out the sex today?" the technician asked.

"No," Paige said. "I want Matt and I to have that surprise together." Paige gave me a watery smile. "You realize what this means though, right?"

"Umm…yes. I do realize how babies are made and where they come from," I said somewhat sarcastically. "It means you're gonna be popping out two babies from your hooha instead of one."

Paige laughed and hit me on my arm. "No, silly. It means I'm going to be the size of one of those Smart cars for your wedding. I won't walk down the aisle in front of you…I'll waddle down." The last part was said on a wail, and I doubled over in laughter.

CHAPTER 3

"Twins. I still can't believe it," I said as we walked toward Paige's roomy SUV. "Do twins run in your family? Because I don't think they run in ours."

"No. No mention of twins in my family. When I first suspected, I dropped a tiny hint to my mom, but she said there are no twins on either her side or dad's side that she knows of."

I buckled my seatbelt then pulled out my phone. "I missed a call while we were in there. Let me get this."

I pulled up my voicemail and heard Samantha Kingston on the other end. I listened to her message then turned to Paige. "That was weird."

"Who was it?" Paige asked as she pulled out of the parking lot.

"Samantha Kingston. I forgot to tell you that Aunt Shirley and I ran into her coming out of the sub shop today. She asked me if I'd come over in the morning to talk with her. She just called again to tell me she's found something important she thinks I need to see. I couldn't exactly hear everything because she was whispering. She said she needed to hurry because she didn't want to get caught."

Paige furrowed her brow. "That's weird she called you. Why wouldn't she just go to Blair with her suspicions and what she's found out?"

I shook my head. "I don't know. Maybe she just wants to run things by me and see what I think before she goes to Blair. Her and Blair seem to be having a difficult relationship right now, so maybe she wants all her ducks in a row."

"I guess you'll find out tomorrow," Paige said.

By the time we made it back to Granville, it was nearly four o'clock. I decided to run by the office real quick to see if anything exciting happened while I was out.

Aunt Shirley and I work at the *Granville Gazette* as reporters. Well, I work as a reporter, Aunt Shirley mostly just takes up space. My Aunt Shirley was a true old maid. She'd never married nor had kids. Instead, she ran away to Los Angeles when she was in her early twenties and became a private investigator. I think she's around seventy-five, but I'm not sure. And she's not telling.

Aunt Shirley has no background in anything other than stakeouts and telling whoppers about how she used to sleep with all the hottest Hollywood men back in the day. But she's a lot of fun, and Hank likes having her around the office.

My boss, Hank Perkins, is a retired Marine who still walks the walk and talks the talk. A "Kill 'Em All, Let God Sort 'Em Out" kinda guy. Once a Marine, always a Marine. Oorah! There are two loves in his life—his wife and his newspaper. In that order.

Mindy was definitely the angel and anchor in the relationship. She was as gentle and kind as he was mean and surly. She had platinum blonde hair that was teased for miles thanks to her old pageant days. She always wore skin-tight Capri pants, neon colored off-the-shoulder shirts or sweaters, and designer high-heeled shoes. She was a true jewel.

Mindy was at her desk filing her nails when I walked into the office. "Hey, sugar, how did the veil thing go?"

I set my purse down on my desk and sighed. "Fine. It was a lot less harrowing than I thought it would be. Anything new happen while I was away?"

"Yeah," Hank hollered from the doorway of his office as he yanked his unlit cigar out of his mouth. "I hired a reporter who's actually gonna show up for work, be here in the office, and do her job!"

I rolled my eyes at Mindy. Same story, different day. Hank always complained I didn't spend enough time in the office, but I've never missed a deadline yet.

"I hope you gave her a crash course on how to survive on peanuts," I yelled back at him. "She's gonna need it."

Hank snorted. "Youth today. You're what's wrong with America...mouthy and ungrateful." He slammed his office door and went back to work.

"You two." Mindy shook her head as I sat down with a huff in my chair. "So today went well?"

"Yeah. I got the veil ordered. One more thing I can check off my list."

"Where's Aunt Shirley?"

"I went ahead and dropped her off at the Manor. She needs to brush up on her self-defense moves before class tomorrow night."

"Hank will be pleased." Mindy got up from her desk and walked toward the display case that held all her herbal teas. "I got just the thing for you. I just got it in. It's supposed to be invigorating and energizing." I really didn't want any tea, but I also didn't want to hurt Mindy's feelings.

24

"I still have that article on the upcoming fair to do this week," I said. "Otherwise, I think I've finished everything else that was due."

Mindy set a cup of piping hot herbal tea in front of me. It was almost ninety degrees outside and she wanted me to drink hot tea. I picked up the tea and blew on it. I had to admit it smelled delicious.

"Wanna hear something weird?" I asked. "While I was having my veil measured by the manager, Samantha Kingston, the owner, Blair Watkins, came in and started chewing her out. It seems Samantha is getting blamed for some problems the store is having. Samantha asked me and Aunt Shirley to meet her tomorrow before the store opens to discuss some of the problems."

Mindy's brow wrinkled. "That *is* weird. Are you going?"

"Yeah. I'm curious about a lot of things. According to her the store is losing money, yet it looks to be doing a good business as far as I can tell." I took a sip of the tea. "Hey, this really is good."

"Told ya. Well, you two girls be careful and try not to get into trouble."

My house is a one-bedroom, eight hundred square foot cottage. It currently sports a faded yellow exterior with white shutters. I put a window box under my one and only window in the front of the house to give it more personality. The porch spans the front of the house and sags dangerously in some places. I love this little house my brother, Matt, rents to me. I'm gonna be sad to see it go when I marry Garrett.

I opened the front door and was immediately greeted by my long-haired black and white tuxedo cat, Miss Molly. Molls loves cat food and being the center of attention. And that's about it.

After feeding Miss Molly, I picked up my cell phone to call Aunt Shirley. I quickly told her about the message Samantha left me and that she found something interesting that I should know about.

"I got a weird feeling about this," Aunt Shirley said. "And you know my gut is never wrong."

I bit my lip to keep from laughing. Aunt Shirley was wrong more often than she was right, but I wasn't going to remind her of that fact.

"I better get off here and go back to my core workout," Aunt Shirley said. "Have you been practicing your moves for class tomorrow night?"

I hadn't, but I wasn't going to admit that to her. "I've been practicing a little. I'll do some more tonight"

"Liar. Hank will kick your butt if you don't take this seriously."

I hung up with Aunt Shirley and went to pour a glass of wine. I was expecting Garrett for dinner in about an hour, and I had yet to set something out.

I rummaged around my near-empty fridge and found some leftover chicken from Sunday night. I gave it the ole sniff test and it smelled fine. Two days in a refrigerator…it *should* be fine. I don't always make the best choices when it comes to deciding whether something is rotten or not.

I got out spinach leaves, olives, cucumbers, radishes, and dried cranberries to go with the chicken, and found some frozen bread in the freezer. I'm really hoping when Garrett and I get married that he'll do a lot of the cooking.

Forty minutes and a glass of wine later, Garrett opened the front door and gave Miss Molly a rub under her chin. He sauntered into the kitchen and gave me a much better greeting hello.

Garrett was thirty-nine, had short black hair left over from his military days, and beautiful dark blue eyes. He also had a boatload of muscles. Sometimes touching him could be pretty intimidating.

"I'd have helped with dinner," he said as he reached in the refrigerator for a beer.

"I know. I just threw a chicken salad together. Does that sound good."

He grinned mischievously at me. "I have a couple of things in mind that sound good."

I swatted him with a dishtowel and laughed. "Dinner first."

He shrugged and took a swig of his beer. "Can't blame me for trying."

"Go get comfortable."

He returned a few minutes later looking more relaxed. He'd taken off his gun belt and uniform and changed into shorts and a black t-shirt. He came up behind me, wrapped his arms around my waist, and nuzzled my neck.

"You got a lot of scruffies on your face," I squealed and tried to squirm out of his hold. "You're feeling pretty frisky there. Good day?"

He gave me a swat on the butt and picked up his beer. "Any day that doesn't have you finding a dead body is a good day."

I stuck my tongue out at him and poured a little more wine in my glass. Just because in eight or so months I'd stumbled across quite a few dead bodies didn't give him the right to razz me.

Okay, maybe it did.

"Grab the bread out of the oven," I commanded as I carried the chicken salad to the table.

We sat down and ate in silence for a few minutes. "Don't forget we have cake tasting at two o'clock tomorrow," I reminded him. "It shouldn't take but an hour or so."

"I remember. Anything going on at the office tomorrow for you?"

I slowly wiped my mouth with a napkin. I knew I had to choose my words carefully. I didn't want to tell Garrett about my meeting with Samantha in the morning, but I didn't want to lie, either. "Not a whole lot. I have one thing I need to get done. Otherwise, it should be a slow day. I'll have no problem getting off at two for the tasting."

Garrett's eyebrows shot up. "Notice I didn't ask you if you could get away or not. I never thought it would be a problem. So, what're you really doing? Anything I need to be concerned about?"

I scowled at him. "No. Just one meeting, that's it. Nothing really."

He gave me a look that said he knew I was lying. Dating— and now marrying—the chief of police does have its drawbacks.

Once the dishes had been done and the table was cleared, we snuggled up on the couch to see what was on TV. No surprise, there was nothing on.

"Want some dessert?" I asked, wiggling my brows.

Garrett grinned and turned off the TV. "Always." He pulled me up off the couch and walked me to the bedroom.

CHAPTER 4

I pulled up to the Manor right at seven and Aunt Shirley hopped in the Falcon. She was looking pretty dapper in bright yellow polyester pants and a button-up shirt with large print daisies. The pastel blue, green, and purple in her hair really captured the outfit.

It only took five minutes to get to Quilter's Paradise. I pulled into the deserted parking lot and drove to the back of the store. I wasn't surprised it was so deserted. Store hours were from eight to five, six days a week…closed on Sundays.

"Samantha said she'd leave the back door open for us. She's supposed to be in the back room like we were in yesterday working on orders."

"I've been thinking about what she's going to tell us today," Aunt Shirley said.

I nodded. "Bad reviews don't really concern me as much as the competing company always knowing what's on sale and the store suddenly losing money."

I parked the Falcon close to the back door and got out. The June sun was already beating down on the black pavement. I waited until Aunt Shirley was behind me before pulling the back door open. I was a little surprised it was unlocked. Even though Samantha said she'd leave it unlocked, a part of me thought she might not really do it. Or maybe I was just feeling weird about entering a store that was closed to customers.

Aunt Shirley let the door bang shut, causing me to jump and let out a little scream. Aunt Shirley chuckled behind me and called me a sissy. The tiny hallway was extremely narrow with two doors leading into the store. I wasn't sure which door to open, so I chose the first one on my right. It looked like a large storeroom. I opened the other door and walked into a brightly lit hallway that I recognized from yesterday. There were three rooms in this part of the store.

"Samantha?" I didn't get an answer. "Samantha, it's Ryli and Aunt Shirley."

"She's probably got those ear bud thingies in and can't hear us," Aunt Shirley said. "I'll look in this room, you take that one."

I nodded and went into the room we were all in yesterday. "Samantha?" No answer and no one was in the room.

"Any luck?" Aunt Shirley hollered.

"No. You?"

"Nope. Let's go check the other room."

I met her in the hallway and we both entered the third room. Empty.

"Oh boy," Aunt Shirley said, her eyes wide. "That doesn't look good."

"What? The room's…" I trailed off because I finally saw what Aunt Shirley did. There was blood splatter across the floor. I followed it to where we were standing. "Maybe she pricked herself with a needle or cut her hand."

Aunt Shirley grunted. "Had to be one heck of a cut. The arterial spray is pretty large."

I hated it when she talked like that. Usually because it meant we were going to find something we didn't want to find.

"Let's follow the blood trail," Aunt Shirley suggested.

"I really don't want to," I mumbled. But I knew the score…it didn't really matter what I wanted when it came to Aunt Shirley.

"Wait." Aunt Shirley grabbed my arm as I turned to walk out the door. She pointed to an overturned box sitting on a shelf in the room. "Go get a pair of those latex gloves real quick. Just in case we need to touch something. I don't want our fingerprints showing up."

My heart leaped. "I don't want to. In fact, I think we should just head out right now." I looked at my watch. "I'd say the morning employees should be arriving within twenty minutes. Let's just come back when the store is open."

"Go get the gloves."

I sighed. I knew what that voice meant and no matter how much I protested, it wouldn't matter. I slowly made my way across the floor—averting my eyes from the blood splatter on the ground. I reached over and turned the box right-side up and then took out two blue gloves.

I glanced down and saw an open purse on the floor…like someone had dropped it and just left it. The purse's contents were strewn all over the floor. At quick glance I noticed lipstick, a wallet, small bottle of hand lotion, sunglasses. What I didn't see was a cell phone.

"There's a spilled purse over here behind the desk," I said. "Normal stuff scattered out of the purse. I don't see a cell phone, though."

"Well, don't touch anything," Aunt Shirley said. "The police can take care of it when they get here."

"Is that your way of saying I should call the police now?" I asked hopefully.

"Looks like the blood trail goes left, out into the store," Aunt Shirley said, obviously ignoring my question.

We followed the drops of blood—which got larger and smeared in some parts of the hallway—out into the main area of the store. The sun poured through the windows, which cause the store to be bright even though the lights were all off.

My eyes locked on a pair of feet sticking out at the end of one of the aisles. "Samantha!"

Aunt Shirley and I ran over to Aisle 4—Thread and Needles. Lying on her side, twisted on the ground, a look of horror frozen on her face, and cutting sheers sticking out of the side of her neck…was Samantha Kingston.

"Get a grip," Aunt Shirley demanded when she saw me go into panic mode. "There's nothing we can do for her right now except find her killer. The blood has started to congeal, which means she's been here awhile. Let's look for clues before we call it in."

"No! Garrett is going to—"

"Give me those gloves then." Aunt Shirley snatched the pair of blue latex gloves out of my hand and shoved her hands into them. She squatted down next to the body, careful not to step in any of the blood. "Looks like she's clutching something in her right hand."

I told myself not to look or get involved, but I couldn't help it. "What is it?"

Aunt Shirley reached out and gently pried the paper out of Samantha's hand and opened the note. "Looks like a piece of torn paper—a ledger of numbers with question marks, notes questioning purchases. I'm not exactly sure what it means, but snap a picture of it with your camera."

I dug my cell phone out of my pocket and did as she demanded. Aunt Shirley then folded the note back up and tucked it back in Samantha's hand.

Aunt Shirley squatted down over Samantha's body. "Other than the hole in the side of her neck, she doesn't look to be stabbed anywhere else on her front. But there's blood down here by her lower back. I bet she's been stabbed a number of times in her back. That's probably why there's larger blood splatter in some areas. The killer probably chased her down the hall and out into the store, stabbing her repeatedly as she ran." Aunt Shirley got up and looked toward the back of the store where we had just come from. "Runs out here, trying to get away from the stabbing and killing, then turns and confronts her killer," Aunt Shirley imitated the actions as she saw them in her mind. "Killer stabs her one more time in the neck, and down she falls. Which explains why her leg is all twisted and broken looking and why she fell face up and sideways instead of face down."

I wiped a tear from my eye. I couldn't even begin to imagine what kind of terror Samantha experienced right before she died. "Can I call Garrett now?"

"Yes."

I was getting ready to dial Garrett's number when I heard the front door bang shut. I walked sideways until I could get a view of who walked through the door. It was the owner, Blair Watkins. She hadn't seen me yet, she was too busy straightening a quilt hanging in the store window.

"Samantha," Blair finally called out. "Are you in the back?"

I didn't want to scare her, so I didn't say anything. My mind was racing on what I'd say to her…how I'd explain our being here when the store was closed…and how I'd explain the dead body we were currently hovered around.

"Blair, is that you?" Aunt Shirley yelled out.

"Yes. Samantha? Your voice sounds weird."

Blair quickly made her way to the back of the store. Her high-heeled shoes making a clicking sound on the linoleum. She stopped short when she saw Aunt Shirley and me standing in the aisle.

"What are you doing here?" Blair demanded. "We aren't open for another thirty minutes or so."

I didn't say anything, just motioned her over. She was probably ten yards out before she looked down and saw Samantha lying on the ground with the sheers stuck in her neck.

Blair let out a blood curdling scream. She took off toward Samantha's body then stopped suddenly. She backtracked and started walking slowly backward, her eyes as huge as saucers. "What have you done?"

Had she slapped me I wouldn't have been more surprised. "We didn't do anything. She called me yesterday and asked me to stop by today before the store opened. She wanted to talk with me."

Blair narrowed her eyes at me and silently studied me. "I don't think so. If she wanted to talk about the veil, she would have asked you to come in during store hours. That's not something she'd do while the store is closed."

I looked at Aunt Shirley, unsure how to proceed. At this point I knew everyone was a suspect—including Blair. How much did we admit to her?

"She wanted to talk with us about a private matter," Aunt Shirley supplied. "When we couldn't find her in the back, we came out here and saw her."

"Where's your car?" Blair demanded. "I didn't see any cars in the parking lot."

"She asked me to park around back and she'd leave the back door open for us," I said.

Fury crossed Blair's face. "Why would she do that? She knows that's against the rules!"

Good manners refrained me from pointing out to Blair that getting mad at Samantha was pointless—she was dead after all.

"I think it's time I called Garrett," I said softly.

"Who's Garrett?" Blair asked. "And why are you calling him and not the police?"

"He is the police," I said. "He's the chief of police for Granville."

I turned away before I totally decked Blair. It was a common reaction I had when dealing with fear and nerves. I hit the send button and waited for Garrett to pick up. He did on the second ring.

"Hey, babe. What's up?"

I swallowed. You'd think this whole I-found-a-dead-body thing would get easier the more I did it, but it didn't. "I stopped by the store where I'm getting my wedding veil made," I said, hoping the added part of wedding would remind him he was marrying me for better or worse, "and I found a dead body." I said that last part really fast. It kinda came out like andIfoundadeadbody.

Silence.

"Please tell me I didn't just hear what I think I did."

I sighed. "You did. Aunt Shirley and I—"

"Why am I not surprised!" Garrett exclaimed. "It's like every story you tell that ends bad starts with 'Aunt Shirley and I.' Have you noticed that?"

I chose to ignore him. I've learned that about Garrett. Usually I have to ignore the first thing out of his mouth when I tell him about discovering a dead body. Otherwise I'd take it personally and totally get my feeling hurt something fierce.

"So anyway, I think you need to get down to Quilter's Paradise immediately." I gave him the address and hung up before he could get good and mad at me.

"He should be here shortly," I informed Aunt Shirley and Blair. I could tell by the scowl on Aunt Shirley's face she'd overheard Garrett's remark about us.

"I can't believe this has happened," Blair said. "I suppose we'll have to shut down for the morning now." She blew out a breath. "This is so inconvenient."

My mouth dropped open. "You realize one of your employees has just been murdered in your store, right?" I knew I sounded like a total witch, but I didn't care.

Blair waved a dismissive hand in my direction. "Of course. It's such a tragedy. But so is the fact that I have a ton of orders I'm not sure how I'm going to get filled with one less hand working on them."

CHAPTER 5

"Let's go over this one more time." Garrett's voice was strained as he ran a hand through his short, black hair. He'd separated me from Aunt Shirley and Blair. He was questioning me, Matt was questioning Aunt Shirley, and Officer Ryan was questioning Blair Watkins.

Willa Trindle was being comforted by one of the EMTs while our coroner, Melvin Collins, was making the pronouncement. Willa had arrived a few minutes after Garrett and the rest of the officers. According to Willa, Lexi Miller, the social media manager, was due any minute now. So was Ronni Reynolds, another employee.

I sighed and went over my story one more time. "I ran into Samantha yesterday at lunch after leaving the store, and she asked me to meet her here this morning. After thinking about it, she said she had some theories about the store and the problems it's undergoing that she wanted to share them with me. Then a few hours later, I received a call from her telling me that she had found something important regarding the store that she wanted me to look at when I came here."

"And you believe she was being set up to fail at this store and what she found last night may have gotten her killed?"

"I'm not one hundred percent sure since I never got the chance to talk with her, but yeah. I think she wanted to talk with me about what I overheard yesterday—you know, when I was picking out my veil for our wedding." I said this last part in hopes of some brownie points. It must not have worked because he motioned me to continue. "She thought someone was either setting her up to make it look like she was doing a bad job or set her up so she was somehow responsible for other companies getting a jump on the store's sale merchandise. Either way, someone was out to get her."

"So you parked in the back like she told you, and then you and Aunt Shirley just walked into the store. Did that not strike you as odd?"

"Not really. She said she'd leave it unlocked."

If I didn't know better, I'd swear there was a small tic developing around Garrett's eye. "What did you do after you entered the store?"

"Like I said, Aunt Shirley and I went to the other rooms in the back where we were yesterday, but they were all empty. In the last room we noticed blood splatter, so we decided to follow it and see where it led." It wasn't exactly the whole story…but close enough.

"Let me get this straight. You see blood splatter and decide to follow it. Not call the police and tell them what you've discovered. You and Aunt Shirley decide it would be a good idea to follow the blood splatter and see where it leads." He didn't make any of it sound like a question, so I didn't reply with an answer. "Please tell me you didn't touch anything—the body or anything around it."

I only hesitated a moment. No way was I telling him the truth. "I didn't touch a thing." Which was the truth. Aunt Shirley was the one that touched the items on the body. "In fact, we were so careful we made sure we didn't step in any of the blood splatter!"

Garrett was definitely sporting a left-eye tic. "Well, thank God for small favors."

I ignored the sarcastic remark. "Then the owner Blair Watkins came in, and at first she thought we had something to do with it. Then when she realized we didn't, she got all witchy and blamed Samantha for ruining the day with her dying because now the store would be closed down. Can you believe that? I think you need to take a closer look at her!"

Garrett grunted. "Being rude doesn't mean you're guilty of anything."

"Doesn't mean you aren't," I countered.

Garrett didn't lift his eyes or even pause from writing in his notebook to acknowledge what I'd said. Once he finished, he closed the pad and stared silently at me. It took everything I had not to fold like a house of cards and admit to anything he wanted. He knew this police tactic usually had me singing like a canary, but I've been working on maintaining nerves of steel when it comes to his interrogations.

Garrett reached out and touched my cheek. "I love you. You know that, right?"

I blinked in surprise. Of all the things he could have said to me, this totally caught me by surprise. Tears filled my eyes. "Of course I know you love me. And you know I love you." I wasn't sure where he was going with this new line of questioning. "What's going on? Why the sudden change in tactic?"

Garrett chuckled softly. "No reason. I just sometimes feel like I'm constantly—not really blaming you for landing in trouble, but I know I get exasperated with you. Especially since I believe Aunt Shirley is the one that usually drags you kicking and screaming into these situations. Deep down I know you can't control the trouble that seems to plague you at every corner, but it doesn't stop me from worrying about you." He shrugged. "So I want to make sure you know I love you. Because chances are I'm going to yell and lose my cool before this mystery is solved."

I grinned and blew him a kiss. "I never doubt your love for me. Does this mean I'm free to go?" I paused and grinned mischievously at him. "And don't worry, Chief, I won't leave town."

Garrett grunted. It was the closest thing I'd get to an acknowledgment that he actually loves my smart mouth. He turned and walked toward Officer Ryan and Blair Watkins. I was going to tell him I'd let him frisk me later, but I didn't think it was an appropriate time…what with Samantha's body being wheeled out of the store and all.

I caught Aunt Shirley's eye across the store and headed her way with a spring in my step. It was the first time ever that Garrett hadn't reminded me to mind my own business, stay out of his way, and let the professionals do their job.

"I was just telling Matt here that I think that Blair Watkins lady may be guilty of something," Aunt Shirley said by way of greeting. "I don't like her or her attitude."

I gave Matt a little pat on the arm and nodded my head at Aunt Shirley. "I tried to tell Garrett the same thing, but he told me being rude doesn't equate to an arrest for murder."

"And that's why he's the Chief," Matt quipped.

"Are you done with Aunt Shirley?" I asked Matt, sneaking a peek over Willa Trindle's way. "I need to get to the office this morning. I haven't texted Hank yet about this, so I'm sure he's faunching at the mouth thinking I'm late."

"You got it, Sis. I'm gonna have to ask you to walk outside and around to the back so you don't disturb the crime scene."

"That's fine." I glanced again at Willa. She was currently alone and leaning against a wall by the front of the store. A perfect opportunity to go feel her out. "I'll see you later."

"Why're you in such a hurry?" Aunt Shirley asked as I grabbed her by the arm and hauled her down the aisle toward the front of the store. "You know Hank isn't going to want to see your face at the office with this kind of scandal going on."

"I know," I said. "I want to go talk with Willa."

Aunt Shirley nodded her head sagely. "Now you're thinking like a P.I."

Willa Trindle was leaning against the wall, texting on her phone, paying no attention to what was going on around her. She was dressed in black pants and a bright red Quilter's Paradise shirt, with her nametag pinned neatly above her left breast pocket.

"Hey, Willa." I stood in front of her and gave her my most sympathetic smile. I was pretty sure she'd already texted half of Granville, posted an emotional status on social media, and maybe even uploaded a picture of herself surrounded by all the chaos. "How're you holding up?"

She smiled brightly and slid her phone in the front pocket of her pants. "Can you believe this? Imagine, a murder at my workplace. I mean, I know this kind of thing seems to happen to you all the time, but this is a first for me. Your poor husband-to-be, how in the world does that handsome man handle all the trouble you seem to get into?"

Not gonna lie, I balled up my fists to keep from scratching her eyes out. "Just one of the many things he loves about me." I heard Aunt Shirley snicker at my reply, but I wasn't going to let Willa get under my skin today.

"Tell me, Willa, what do you know of the problems the store's having?" Aunt Shirley asked. "I bet you know more than anyone."

Willa preened at Aunt Shirley, taking her remark for a compliment. "Well, I actually know—"

"What's going on here?" I turned and saw a beautiful woman trying to push her way through the throng of EMTs standing by the front door. "Let me through. I work here."

"That's Lexi," Willa stated.

I caught the eye of Steven Vaugh, an EMT who was hovering by the door, and tilted my head to let him know to bring the woman over to us. He looked around to see if anyone was either going to help him or stop him—not sure which—before leading Lexi to where Aunt Shirley, Willa, and I were standing.

Lexi Miller was a strikingly beautiful woman with waist-length straight black hair and dark brown almond eyes. Her nose was small and her lips were pouty and full. There wasn't a single wrinkle on her face.

"Willa, what is going on here?" She didn't even bother addressing Aunt Shirley or me. I guess she figured she'd get more answers from Willa.

"It's terrible," Willa said. Only, she didn't exactly sound like it was terrible. She sounded like she was excited. "Samantha has been murdered!"

Lexi Miller blinked a couple times and waited…as if she expected a punch line to follow. "Murdered? Are you sure?"

I nodded my head. "We're sure. My aunt and I found her this morning."

Lexi looked me up and down and then frowned. "Who are you? And why are you here before the store is scheduled to open?"

"I'm Ryli Sinclair, and this is Aunt Shirley. Samantha contacted me yesterday and asked me to come in early today. She wanted to speak with me."

"Talk with you about what?" Lexi asked.

"Store problems," Aunt Shirley supplied. "She thought my niece and I could help."

"That makes no sense. Why would she tell strangers about what's going on?" Lexi frowned at us. "And how could you help?"

"Lexi!" Blair cried from the back of the store.

It was like the fight suddenly went out of Blair when she saw Lexi. Her face crumbled and she started sobbing. Garrett took her by the arm and led her down the length of the store to where we were all standing. When Garrett and Blair got within ten feet of us, Blair wrenched free and ran to Lexi, throwing her arms around the startled woman.

"What's this about Samantha being murdered?" Lexi asked. "I can't believe this!"

"I know," Blair wailed. "The last thing the store needs is this kind of publicity! And now I've been told that the store has to be closed today. This is so inconvenient."

44

"Um, yes." I could tell Lexi was taken aback by Blair's attitude as much as we all were. "Have you spoken with Daniel yet? Does he know?"

"No," Blair said and wiped her eyes. "I can't seem to reach him. I've left two messages on his phone, but goodness only knows where that man is."

I surreptitiously looked at Aunt Shirley. Her raised eyebrow let me know she was just as interested in this little bit of news as I was.

"Once we locate Daniel, you'll feel better," Lexi said soothingly. "I'm sure it's just your nerves talking."

I shot Garrett a pointed look, but he chose to ignore me. Guess he was still holding firm to the ridiculous belief that being a heartless witch didn't make you a murderer.

CHAPTER 6

"I'm really sorry about this," Garrett said as he ran a finger down my neck. He decided to walk Aunt Shirley and me back to the Falcon. Guess he didn't want us getting into any more trouble. "Should we cancel, or do you want to go ahead with the cake tasting you had scheduled today?"

I sighed. I really had no idea what I wanted to do. We were four months out before the wedding, surely another week or two wouldn't matter if we canceled our cake-tasting appointment today.

"How about I call Barbara and see what she thinks. After all, she's the one making the cake and knows how much time she needs. If she really needs us today, I'll take Mom and Paige with me and let the cake be a surprise for you."

Garrett grunted. "Did you really think I wouldn't notice you left out Aunt Shirley in that scenario. I'm not thrilled with the prospect of her picking out our wedding cake."

Don't worry," I laughed. "Everything will be fine. Like I said, I'll call Barbara and see what her thoughts are about today. I'll text you and let you know what we decide."

"Thanks. I can reply to a text faster than I can a phone call." He leaned in and brushed a kiss across my ear. "Again, I'm sorry. But I promise to make it up to you. Stay at my house tonight?"

I grinned wickedly at him. "Like you need to ask." I barely refrained from melting into the parking lot pavement. "I may be a little late, though. Aunt Shirley and I have our self-defense class at the Manor tonight."

Garrett rolled his eyes. "I still can't believe Oak Grove Manor is promoting this class, and that Hank agreed to teach it."

Truth is, ever since the double murder a few months back, the Manor had to make some pretty substantial changes due to a decrease in enrollment. Since then, they've added an aquatic pool, a couple weight machines, and a self-defense class.

Aunt Shirley stuck her head out the passenger-side window. "Let's move it you two. We need to write up an article for the paper."

"I'd say keep me posted on how it's going here," I said, "but you and I both know you won't."

"Goodbye, Ryli."

I hopped in the Falcon and drove us back to the office. Aunt Shirley was scribbling away on a pad, so I left her alone until she finished up.

"I like your hair," I said once she was done. "I don't know if I told you that or not."

Aunt Shirley put a hand up to her head and patted her hair into place. "Thanks. I know I usually do a bright color, but this time I was feeling softer. I really like the pastel colors."

Aunt Shirley has a different hairstyle and hair of color nearly every month. This month it was cut into a chin-length bob with pastel purple, green, and blue streaked throughout. It was more color than she usually did, but since the cut was more subtle than normal, it was a good balance.

I glanced down her body. "You're looking pretty buff in the arms, too."

Aunt Shirley grinned and flexed her muscles. "I'm loving this swimming pool. I swim about twenty laps a night!"

"Well, it looks good on you."

Aunt Shirley beamed with pride.

Mindy was on the phone when we walked in the office. She held up a finger to let us know she'd only be a minute. I looked over at Hank's closed door. I wasn't sure what to make of that. I figured the minute we walked in he'd storm out and demand to know what we knew about Samantha's murder.

I wasn't disappointed. A few seconds later Hank's door opened. He leaned against the door jamb and yanked his unlit cigar from his mouth. "Whatcha got?"

"I wrote down things we know so far," Aunt Shirley said. "Wanna hear them?"

Mindy got up from her desk. "Yes. But let me get us some lavender mint green tea. Something tells me we need to get our thinking caps on, and mint's just the thing to do it."

"So's whiskey," Aunt Shirley joked, "but you never seem to have that here at the office."

Aunt Shirley and Hank guffawed over that while Mindy rolled her eyes and went to make some hot tea. A few minutes later, Mindy set our tea down in front of us and we all scooted our chairs together to mull over the victim and the motives we had so far.

"Victim is Samantha Kingston," Aunt Shirley said. "She believed someone was either setting her up to take the fall for the company failing, or someone was targeting her so she'd fail and lose her job. She called us to come in early today because she believed she either found something to corroborate her assumption or something along those lines. We aren't sure which."

"Suspects?" Hank demanded.

I sighed. "That's a little harder. I'd say definitely all the workers at the Quilter's Paradise store—even though we haven't met everyone yet."

"What do you mean?" Mindy asked.

"There are only six workers," I said. "Well, five now that Samantha is dead. We know that Blair's husband, Daniel, does the bookkeeping for both stores, but no one can locate him right now. Also, there's another employee, Ronni Reynolds, who was due at the store but never arrived. So the first person on the list is Willa Trindle. I'd say her motive would be she'd do anything to get Samantha's job as manager. Maybe with the fighting going on between Blair and Samantha, she saw it as an opportune time to kill Samantha and try to take her job."

"Do you really think she'd go so far as to kill someone?" Mindy asked.

Aunt Shirley shrugged. "Who knows. We've all seen crazier things over these last few months."

"Then you have Lexi Miller, the social media manager," I continued. "I'm not sure of her motive. Maybe Lexi and Samantha got into a fight about the store or something like that."

Aunt Shirley scrunched her nose. "Weak."

I rolled my eyes. "Not if Samantha and Lexi got into a fight over the issues of the store. Let's say one of them found out that the other has been telling the competitor in Kansas City what the sale items are for the week."

"Keep going with that," Hank said. "Was something going on between competitive stores?"

I explained how Samantha told us that the competitor always seemed to know what the sale items were for the weekend and how the store was being hit hard by negative reviews.

Hank whistled. "Corporate espionage?"

"What's that?" I asked.

"Basically, someone from a competitive company may approach someone who works for the company they are trying to sabotage and offers to give the person money or a better job within their company in exchange for information that can cripple the competition. Think about it. That theory makes sense as to why the competitive company knows what's going to be on sale early, and maybe the competitive company is writing the bad reviews with the help of the company spy for Quilter's Paradise."

"You're thinking Samantha was the spy?" I asked incredulously.

Hank shrugged. "I didn't say that. Maybe she was the spy and the killer found out. They thought the best way to deal with it was to kill her. Or maybe Samantha found out who the spy was and she confronted him or her and they decided to kill her."

Aunt Shirley nodded. "I'd say it's a pretty good bet that the piece of paper clutched in Samantha's dead hand had something to do with the murder."

"What paper?" Hank demanded as he scowled at me. "I said I wanted to know everything."

I blew out my breath exasperatingly. "I was getting to that. Geez! We found a torn piece of paper in Samantha's hand that showed numbers that were circled, notes in the margins." I dug out my phone from my pocket and pulled up the photo.

Hank whistled. "That doesn't look good for the person who keeps the books."

I smiled. "Next we come to Daniel Watkins, Blair's husband. He's the accountant for both stores. And like I said before…evidently no one can locate him."

"Definitely not good," Mindy agreed and took a drink of her tea.

"He's definitely a prime suspect," Aunt Shirley said.

"Then we have the owner, Blair Watkins," I said. "I'm not sure what her motive would be, especially since it's her company that's suffering. I can't see her sabotaging her own store. So maybe she killed Samantha because she found out Samantha actually *was* the corporate spy."

"And who's the last person?" Mindy asked.

"Ronni Reynolds. I'm not sure what her motive would be seeing as how we've never even met her, much less spoken to her about anything going on at the store."

"I say you start where you can," Hank said, "and ask a lot of questions. Maybe see who has profitably gained over the last few months. Look around their houses—anyone driving a new car they can't explain? I'm sure someone will crack eventually. Good job today. Now, get to work!"

He turned and walked back to his office and slammed his door closed.

"Where do you want to start?" Aunt Shirley asked.

"First thing I'm doing is calling Barbara Carole to see about the cake tasting Garrett and I were supposed to do today. Get her opinion on whether or not it would be okay to cancel and reschedule, or should I just go ahead and do it alone."

"You won't be alone," Aunt Shirley said. "I'll go pick out your wedding cake."

Mindy choked on her tea but tried to recover so she didn't hurt Aunt Shirley's feelings. "I think—I mean, I would go, too. This way you'd have another vote."

I smiled gratefully at Mindy. "And I'm sure Mom and Paige would want to go, too."

Aunt Shirley stuck out her bottom lip. "Well, poo. It's not like I can't pick out a wedding cake!"

I wasn't so sure about that. And I can guarantee Garrett would object. "Let me call Barbara real quick."

CHAPTER 7

My text message notification went off around four. I picked up my phone and read a text from Garrett. He'd be at my house around dinnertime for a bite to eat. I still hadn't made it to the store, so I had nothing in my fridge to prepare. I had just planned on eating cereal. I was still at the office, but I'd just emailed my article to Hank so I was free to go.

I took Aunt Shirley home around four-thirty with a promise to see her later on for self-defense class. That left me thirty minutes to get to the grocery store, pick something up, and take it back to my house to prepare.

I pulled up to my house around five-fifteen. Just my luck I ran into four or five different people at the grocery store who wanted to talk about the murder. Grabbing the groceries, I made my way to the front door.

"I was just coming out to help," Garrett said as he walked out of my house, kissed me hello, and took the bag out of my arms.

"Sorry I'm late. I should have known people would have heard about Samantha by now and would want to gossip."

"No worries. What did you get to eat?"

I laughed at his one-track mind. I followed Garrett into the kitchen and turned on the oven. He opened the frozen lasagna dinner and shoved it into the oven then turned on the timer.

"Um, you have to let it preheat, you nut!" I laughed. "You can't be *that* hungry!"

Garrett's eyes darkened and his pupils dilated. "Oh, I am. But not for food."

My mouth went dry as he lifted me over his shoulder like a sack of potatoes. Opening my bedroom door, Miss Molly scampered in behind us and jumped up on the bed.

"Sorry, girl. Not this time," Garrett chuckled as he lifted her off the bed and set her in the hallway and quickly closed the door. Angry meows echoed throughout the house.

"She's not having any of it," I giggled as I wiggled back higher up the bed.

He grinned wolfishly at me. "I'll make it up to her."

"I'm glad we could reschedule the cake tasting today," Garrett said as he poured us each a glass of milk. We stuck with milk since I still had to go to self-defense class later tonight and Garrett was going back to the station.

"Please. There was no way I was going to let Aunt Shirley pick out our cake."

Garrett chuckled. "And I thank you for that small favor."

I grinned saucily up at him. "I thought you did just thank me?"

Garrett let out a full-blown laugh at my joke. "That's true." He took a bite of his lasagna, letting the steam escape his mouth. "This hits the spot. I didn't stop for lunch today."

"I know this is probably a silly question—this being Granville and not a major city—but were there any cameras in the store?"

Garrett arched one eyebrow and gave me a knowing look. "I'll answer this one question, but only this question."

I wavered between a pout and a scowl. I hated when he got all "cop superior" on me.

"The answer is no. The only thing they have is conveniently placed mirrors in the store. No cameras."

"Darn. But I guess that would have been too easy."

Garrett chuckled and shoved another bite of lasagna in his mouth. "True."

Garrett's cell phone registered a text message. He pulled it up and read it. "Looks like Samantha's fiancé will be at the station in about an hour."

Samantha had a fiancé? Poor guy. I need to talk with him soon.

"Are you coming out to my place tonight after your self-defense class?" Garrett asked.

"I better not. I need to be at the office bright and early tomorrow, and I sometimes have a hard time leaving your place on time. I just wanna stay there and drink your fancy coffee and veg out all day."

Garrett looked at me serious-like. It made me squirm in my seat. "You know if you want to quit working after we get married I'm okay with that, right?"

I opened my mouth to tell him as a feminist I was truly insulted that he would think I should stay home all day. Unfortunately, nothing came out. Mainly because a part of me was touched that he cared enough about my happiness that he'd think nothing of me contributing to our relationship in a different way than what we had now. "I appreciate the offer, but I'll probably still work. I'm sure the new at your place will eventually wear off."

Garrett shrugged. "Suit yourself. I just wanted to put the offer out there."

I leaned over and kissed him. He tasted like tomato sauce and garlic. "I know. And I appreciate it. I'll call you tonight to tell you how the class went."

Garrett downed the last of his milk. "Can't wait. Thanks for dinner, but I gotta go. Officer Ryan needs to be relieved."

After Garrett left, I washed the dishes then changed from my work clothes into my workout clothes. I yanked on a pair of black yoga pants with a black and purple Lycra workout shirt, pulled my hair up into a messy bun on top of my head, then laced up my athletic shoes.

I thought about what Garrett had said about quitting my job and staying home, and I couldn't believe how contradicted I felt. I loved my job. I love the freedom I have with it, I love the fact that even though I gripe about it, I get to work with Aunt Shirley. I love writing articles and columns that I know people read and talk about.

On the other hand, I knew the score with Garrett. He was going to be forty soon, and he wanted nothing more than to start a family, which scared me to death. How exactly was I going to continue doing what I do—skulk around and solve murders behind Garrett's back—with a baby on my hip? I wasn't, which meant I had to grow up...which scared me a whole lot more than being held captive at gunpoint.

I gave myself a little shake and grabbed my car keys. I still had a good thirty minutes before class started, but I figured I'd spend the time with Aunt Shirley in the locker room. She usually spent most evenings swimming in the heated saltwater pool the Manor had recently installed.

There were so many cars at the Manor that I couldn't find a parking space in the visitor's section. I drove the Falcon to the side of the building and found parking there. Grabbing my tote bag I hustled inside and went straight for the women's locker room.

I've only been in the women's locker room once before at last month's self-defense class. Take it from me, nothing can prepare you for the sight of eighty-year-old women walking around completely naked.

Let me say that again…completely naked! These women don't give two hoots who sees them. They don't care who sees their flaws. Nope, they just let the saggy boobs hang and they don't care.

I pulled open the locker room door and was immediately greeted by Rose Peterman. She was bone thin, and if she was a day under ninety I'd eat my toes. I tried averting my gaze as she gave her naked body a little shake to get the water off of her. Things went flapping in the wind that had no business flapping. It was weird. You'd think for a skinny old woman she'd have nothing on her that could flap—you'd be wrong.

"Do you need a towel," I asked weakly. "I can probably get you one."

"Why?" Rose asked as she donned a flowered mumu that was four sizes too big. "This here dress will absorb any water."

I thanked the good Lord the dress was so large. It helped hide the fact Rose wasn't wearing any undergarments under the dress. I shook my head in amazement at the fact there didn't seem to be a dress code of any kind at the Manor.

"Your aunt is finishing up her laps right now," Rose said as she gathered up her tote bag and hobbled out of the locker room. She turned and popped her head back in. "Will I see you tonight at self-defense class?"

"Yep. Been practicing my holds."

"Ditto. I even watched some videos online to really get the moves down."

I chuckled at that image. "I'll see ya there."

I made my way out to the pool area. Not only had the Manor splurged on an indoor heated saltwater pool, but they also installed a twenty-person hot tub. I could hear the jets from the hot tub before I even made it out of the back of the locker room.

I saw Aunt Shirley in her fire-engine red bathing suit with matching swim cap effortlessly cutting through the water in the last lane. I walked over and sat down on the bench in front of the lane, not wanting to disturb her.

Movement out of the corner of my right eye had me turning. I barely suppressed the scream that bubbled up in my throat. Coming straight for me was Old Man Jenkins...in a neon green Speedo!

He looked like a hairless cat, thanks in part to the fact he had absolutely no hair on his chest and protruding stomach, nor anywhere else on his skinny, wrinkled body. He had a huge grin plastered on his face as he made his way over to where I sat. He was oblivious to the fact his Speedo was hanging *dangerously* low on his saggy body. And I do mean *dangerously* low.

Note to self...change all of Garrett's underwear to boxers when he reaches a certain age.

"Ryli, honey, how you doing?" Old Man Jenkins asked as he sat down next to me on the bench—his wet body making a plopping sound.

I gritted my teeth and stifled the urge to scoot all the way over on my side of the bench so as not to touch him. I loved Old Man Jenkins, I really did. But I was seeing way more of him than a person should ever have to, especially considering I wasn't his wife.

"I love coming out here and hanging out in the hot tub while your aunt swims her laps. She's so amazing, isn't she?"

I smiled at Old Man Jenkins' wistful voice. The man was so gaga over Aunt Shirley it wasn't even funny. He's been chasing her for at least nine months that I know of. Maybe even before that if I asked him.

"She sure is." I tilted my head backward so I wouldn't be tempted to slide my eyes over his body again. "You swimming laps, too?"

He laughed. "Nope. I just like to make sure I'm out and about walking around when your aunt finishes so she can see all the man she's missing out on by not marrying me."

My head whipped around in his direction. "You want to marry Aunt Shirley?" I couldn't keep the shock out of my voice.

Old Man Jenkins nodded his head. "I sure do. I bet I ask her every day. But every day she gives me some different excuse."

"Can I ask how old you are?"

Mr. Jenkins laughed. "I'm eighty-five years old. Does that surprise you?"

Yes!

"No. I would have guessed you to be around that age."

Plus ten years.

He patted my knee. "Well, looks like your aunt is finishing up. I better stand up and walk away so she can ogle my butt."

Oh, boy!

"What did that crazy old coot want?" Aunt Shirley demanded as she grabbed up her towel and tried off.

"He told me he'd like to marry you," I said incredulously.

Aunt Shirley stopped drying off and stared at me. "Of course he does. I'm a good catch. I may not have my own teeth, but I do have my own place, I don't need a walker to get around, and I got a pretty rockin' body."

I guess it's true what they say—it's all about perspectives.

"I saw Rose Peterman in the locker room," I said as Aunt Shirley and I walked back into the locker room. "She said she watched a bunch of online videos this week to prepare for tonight's self-defense class."

Aunt Shirley rolled her eyes. "That could be dangerous. Make sure you don't get teamed up with her tonight."

I nodded sagely. "Got it."

"Did you practice your different ways to get out of holds?" Aunt Shirley asked.

"Yes. I'll be fine. How hard can it be? You yank your hand back."

Aunt Shirley looked at me with disgust. "Don't you dare try to team up with me."

The locker room was state-of-the-art with showers, lockers, and hair dryers. Aunt Shirley jumped in the shower then dressed in yoga pants, t-shirt, and tennis shoes.

"I think we should run by Quilter's Paradise tomorrow morning," Aunt Shirley said as she finished lacing up her shoes. "Maybe see what's going on. Ask some questions."

I shrugged. "Sounds good to me. I'm kinda hoping we'll hear if the elusive husband, Daniel, has been found yet."

"He's beginning to sound more and more guilty," Aunt Shirley agreed.

"Hey, I forgot to tell you…Samantha was engaged to be married. The fiancé should be at the station talking with Garrett right now."

Aunt Shirley tsked and shook her head. "Poor boy. We'll definitely want to speak with him as soon as we can. He'll have a lot of information for us. Pick me up at eight tomorrow morning. We'll get there right as the store opens."

CHAPTER 8

We walked in the small work-out room the Manor now had with ten minutes to spare. There were about eight women stretching out and getting ready for class. I was the youngest by far. The closest person to my age would have been Myrtle Adams.

I'd place her at seventy. She's relatively new to the Manor and a lot of fun to be around since she's so young. When I asked her why she wanted to live at Oak Grove Manor, she told me it seemed like a lot more fun than living by herself in her house. Her daughter lived in Kansas City and had her own family and didn't get out to see her much. So she decided to sell her place and moved into the Manor.

"Let's go, Ginger Snaps," Hank Perkins yelled and clapped his hands together. "Get your geriatric butts over here."

We all ran to the mat and waited expectantly for instructions. And, yes, I'm well aware I wasn't a geriatric. Hank took a few moments to analyze us as he paced back and forth. Tonight he was wearing camouflage cargo pants with a green t-shirt tucked inside his pants. The outfit showed off how truly fit and athletic he still was even though his Marine days were long over. He stopped pacing in front of Myrtle.

"I expect you all practiced getting out of your holds this week?"

We all nodded our heads expectantly.

"Good. Let's see it. Split up into groups."

I looked at Aunt Shirley, but she shook her head. "Ain't happening. This is serious business. I need someone who really practiced."

"I did!" I hissed.

Aunt Shirley gave me a knowing look.

"How about it?" Rose Peterman asked. "Wanna be my partner, Ryli?"

What could I say? "Of course I do."

I squared up with Rose and we went over the first hold. I was to grab her arm and she simply brings it up by her ear and my grasp is released from her arm. Pretty easy. We took turns practicing the hold and being firm with our voices when we told our assailant to get away.

"Good job, buttercups. Now let's try the one where you add the upswing of your other hand and pretend to hit your assailant in the nose." He stopped in front of me. "Watch me demonstrate. Sinclair, grab my arm."

I'm not gonna lie...I was terrified to grab hold of Hank. Mainly because I wasn't sure he would fake hit me in the nose.

He scowled at me. "You got wax in your ears? I said grab hold of me, Nancy Drew."

I sighed and reached for his arm. In the blink of an eye he had me stumbling back and blinking. He'd been so fast knocking my hand away and bringing his other hand up to my face, the only thing I could do was stumble back.

"Just like that. Even if you don't connect, it will still startle your attacker. But trust me, you make that connection in a time of crisis, your bad guy will be doubled over in pain. Now break up and try it."

I squared up again with Rose. "You wanna go first or do you want me to?"

She gave me a shy smile. "Why don't you go first. This way I can watch you. Even though I watched the moves on the computer, I'm still so nervous about some of this stuff."

Rose slowly reached out to grab my arm and I carefully yanked my arm back, yelled out no, and brought my other hand up to her face, pretending to hit her in the nose.

"Good job, dear," Rose said. "You really had me scared."

I bit back the laughter that wanted to erupt. I knew Hank wouldn't tolerate anyone having fun. "Okay. Now I'll grab your arm and you pretending to hit me in the nose."

Rose nodded. "Got it."

I carefully grabbed hold of her cool, wrinkled arm and pretended to yank her toward me. Unfortunately, I wasn't careful enough, because Rose lost her footing and stumbled into me at the same time she'd brought her hand up to my face. The end of her palm caught me in the nose.

I cried out in pain as stars literally danced behind my closed eyelids. I bent over at my waist and begged God to make the pain stop. I tentatively reached up and touched my nose. Blood greeted me. I recognized Aunt Shirley's snicker even as I was doubled over in pain.

"Oh, dear," Rose exclaimed. "I'm so sorry, Ryli. I lost my footing. Are you okay?"

"She's fine," Hank grumbled as he lifted my upper torso back into a standing position. I fought against the lightheadedness I felt. No way was I fainting at Hank's feet. He'd never let me live it down.

"Move your hands," he commanded. "Lemme see."

I held my face up for him to examine. "How bad is it?"

"You'll live."

He turned his back on me and walked away. My nostrils flared. I wanted to knock him on his butt so badly, I could hardly breathe.

"I can hear your thoughts, Sinclair," Hank hollered with his back still to me. "Mind you don't do anything rash."

I gave him a rude finger gesture. Rose tittered and my bruised ego and nose were momentarily bolstered.

"Are you okay?" Rose asked again. "I'm so sorry. Why don't we just take a break?"

I slid my glance over to Aunt Shirley. She was paired with Myrtle and both ladies were making the moves look effortless and smooth. No way was I taking a break and letting her one-up me.

"I'm fine," I said. "Let's keep going until Hank calls for something else."

The rest of the holds went smoothly, and by the time Hank called for a rest, my nose had stopped stinging. I caught a glimpse of myself in the mirror and cringed. Not only was my nose red, but it looked like my left eye was turning purple.

"Gather round, ladies," Hank called as he took a relaxed military stance in front of us. We fell into place in line and waited expectantly once again. "This next move will be done in two parts. I'm going to teach you how to fling your assailant over your shoulder."

Chaos erupted around me. The old ladies were cackling and clapping at the thought of throwing someone over their shoulder. I had to wonder why the heck Hank would show these ladies a move like that. Seemed to me they'd break a hip or throw their back out.

Hank held up a hand to stop the talking. "You guys did such a great job with the holds, I figured you could handle this next move. Sinclair, over here now." I groaned inwardly. Obviously being the youngest person in the room meant I was going to be used as the dummy every time.

"Stand right here." He placed me where he wanted me. "Again, tonight we are just going to do the first part. I'm going to step in right here, jut out my hip, and Ryli will naturally fall over my shoulder. Now, next month I'll teach you how to flip."

Oomph!

I blinked and realized I was on my back and having difficulty breathing. I turned my head and saw all the old ladies jumping up and down, giggling, and cheering once again. Without warning, Hank had flipped me over.

A thousand ways to hurt him flew through my mind. Just as quickly they flittered away. This was Hank. The man had been trained to kill someone just by pressing on certain body parts. No way was I really going to hurt him, but it made me feel good thinking about it.

"Pair up!"

I curled up on my side and pushed myself up off the mat and hobbled over to Rose. She looked excited, which immediately scared me.

"Don't worry, Ryli. This is the move I watched over and over again on the computer." Rose's geriatric shoes made no noise as she bent her knees like she was warming up. "I know I can do the first part, no problem. In fact, it may sound silly, but I've been

66

lifting weights in preparation for learning this move. I can't wait to fling someone over my shoulder!"

Will this night never end?

"Since I know how to do this," Rose continued, "why don't you go first so I can help you out."

I sighed and turned my body into Rose. I placed my hands where they needed to be and then jutted my hip out like Hank had instructed. Rose fell gently over my back and shoulder. Piece of cake.

"Change partners!" Hank called out.

Rose clapped her hands in glee as she got into position. I was suddenly having second thoughts of this frail old woman flinging me up onto her back.

"I don't want to hurt you, Rose," I said. "I'm afraid I'll fall too hard on your back or you won't have the strength to pull me up over your shoulder."

"I'll use all my strength. It should be okay."

Rose grabbed hold of my arm and jutted her hip into my stomach. My intent was to just lightly drape over her back…unfortunately, the old broad had way more strength than either one of us realized. Next thing I knew, I was once again flying through the air.

Oomph!

The breath left my body and my head started to pound. I closed my eyes and prayed for death. I could hear Aunt Shirley laughing as Rose made all kinds of sympathy noises at me.

"That's class!" Hank hollered. I opened one eye. He was glaring down at me and shaking his head. "Pathetic, Sinclair."

★★★

I was shocked to see Garrett's vehicle in my driveway as I parked the Falcon next to his truck. I was pretty sure we'd decided to stay at our own places tonight. I glanced in the rear-view mirror to see how my face looked. I groaned. It looked like I'd taken a severe beating.

I opened the front door and Miss Molly immediately greeted me. I leaned down to give her a scratch behind her ear. Garrett was on the couch, feet propped up, watching a baseball game.

"Hey, babe. How'd it go ton—"

With an oath, Garrett sprang up from the coach and reached me in two strides. "What happened? Were you attacked?" He turned my head to the side and examined my profile.

"I'm fine. I just got the crap kicked out of me by Rose Peterman."

Garrett blinked at me in confusion. "Isn't she like ninety years old?"

"Shut up. Just shut up."

I pushed past him and went into my tiny kitchen to pour me a stiff drink. I needed it after tonight. I could hear Garrett chuckling as he followed me into the kitchen.

"It's not funny," I shot back. "I'm probably going to have a black eye tomorrow."

Garrett reached in and grabbed a bag of frozen peas out of the freezer. "Here. Put this on your eye and go sit on the couch. I'll bring you a drink."

I grumbled good-naturedly, pleased with the fact I was finally getting some sympathy. I put my feet up on the coffee table and gently placed the peas over my left eye.

"Here you go." Garrett set a tumbler in my hand.

I removed the peas and took a tentative sip. Nice and strong, just how I liked my whiskey if I have to drink whiskey.

"Now, tell me all about it," Garrett grinned. "And please don't leave out any of the good parts."

CHAPTER 9

"You look like you've gone ten rounds with a boxer and lost," Aunt Shirley hooted as she plopped down in the front seat of the Falcon. "Rose really did a number on you."

I glanced up at the rear-view mirror and tried not to cringe. As much as I hated to admit it, she was right. Overnight had not been kind to my face. The hit to my nose caused a small portion under my left eye to turn purplish green. I'd tried to cover it with makeup, but seeing as how I mostly wear mascara and flavored lip balms, I failed miserably.

"I think the first thing we need to do," I said, "is run by Quilter's Paradise and see if we can't get quotes about the murder from employees or customers. This will allow us to find out if the owner's husband, Daniel, was ever found and if anyone knows anything more about the murder."

"Sounds good to me. I've had some theories about the paper that was clutched in Samantha's hand, and it looks really bad for Daniel since he's the book keeper."

I nodded and pulled onto the road that would take us to Quilter's Paradise. "I agree. But it doesn't explain how the competition is getting vital information from Quilter's Paradise."

Aunt Shirley turned in her seat to stare at me. "You think it's two separate actions? I can get behind that, except for the fact that the end result is the same...Quilter's Paradise is being financially ruined."

I blew out a breath. "I honestly don't know what to think right now. This whole thing is bizarre. I mean, corporate espionage? In our tiny town. It just seems odd."

"I did some Internet research last night after our self-defense class, and I learned a lot of useful information when it comes to dispensing the information in a way that the bad guy won't get caught. It was really interesting."

Another addition to the Manor's overhaul was the addition of a computer lab. Aunt Shirley said one of the high school kids comes out and teaches the seniors general uses for computers like how to send and retrieve email, how to get on social media sites, and how to go on different search engines.

"I know we have to get quotes and crap like that for the newspaper," Aunt Shirley said, "but I want to focus today on interviewing suspects. I want to know their impressions of what was going on with Samantha, and what is currently going on in the store. The two employees that live in town, Willa Trindle and Ronni Reynolds, I want to go by their house and see what's what. One of the things I learned last night was that this whole corporate espionage stuff really pays well, just like Hank said."

I pulled into the parking lot of Quilter's Paradise and cut the engine. The store had only been opened five minutes, but already the lot was full of cars. One thing about small-town murders, everyone wants a piece of the action. Especially the nosy and gossipy citizens.

Aunt Shirley tsked. "I recognize Claire Hickman's car over there." Claire was the dispatcher for the Granville Police Department. She believed it was basically her right as the dispatcher to have her nose into everything.

It was bustling inside the store when Aunt Shirley and I entered. A few customers called out to us as we made our way toward the back of the store. I figured Blair would probably be in her office.

"Hello, ladies," Claire Hickman said as she pushed her cart over to where we were. "The store is lively this morning."

Claire usually works the night shift as the dispatcher at the station. She must have set her alarm early to get here right as the store opened. She almost always wore a crushed velour jogging suit of some kind in a bright color. Today was no different except since it was so hot outside, she traded in her crushed velour pants for crushed velour shorts.

I have no idea where Claire finds these outfits of hers. I'd never seen the likes of velour shorts before on anyone else, especially a grown adult who was just as big around as she was tall. It was definitely a scary sight.

"What are you shopping for?" I asked politely.

"Oh, nothing really. I just wanted to check out how things were going down here." Claire glanced over her shoulder before leaning toward us. "There was a lot of activity at the station yesterday evening from what I heard. I'm assuming Garrett told you?"

This is where things get sticky. Claire is of the belief that since Garrett and I are getting married, he tells me everything that goes on at the police station. She couldn't be more wrong. He's still as closed-mouthed as he was when I first met him nearly two years ago. The added perk of sleeping with him didn't gain me anything outside of the bedroom.

I racked my brain trying to remember what he'd told me was even going on at the station yesterday evening. "Oh, you mean that Samantha's fiancé was at the station?"

Claire nodded. "Yes. Poor boy is so distraught. When he left the station last night, he told me he was staying in town at the Granville Hotel."

Good to know. That should be our next stop.

The Granville Hotel was really more of a motel located in one of the storefront buildings downtown. Way back in the day, when those type of building hotels were popular to stay in, I was told it was a grand place, with lots of polished wood and plush carpets inside. Now it was more of a desperate decision travelers had to make, seeing as how there really wasn't another place in town for visitors to stay.

"I'm sure Garrett will have this case solved quickly," I said. "Samantha's fiancé shouldn't have to stay there long."

Claire's face turned red. "You caught me. I do know more."

"Spill it," Aunt Shirley demanded.

Claire lowered her voice. "It seems the owner's husband, Daniel Watkins, has been up to some shifty stuff. I don't know specifics, but I know Garrett is looking at him hard." Claire glanced around the store quickly. "In fact, I'm surprised Garrett's not here already. From what I understand, Daniel told him he'd be at the store in the morning if Garrett needed to speak with him further."

I sucked in a breath. "Is Garrett thinking Daniel is the murderer?"

"I'm not sure," Claire said. "But I wanted to make sure I was here this morning just in case something went down."

Aunt Shirley tugged on my arm. "C'mon. We need to move quickly if Garrett is on his way."

I said good-bye to Claire and rushed after Aunt Shirley. She was right, if Garrett was headed our way, we needed to pick up the pace. As we entered the back of the store where I'd recently been measured for my wedding veil, I saw Lexi Miller working in one of the rooms.

Aunt Shirley and I paused outside Blair's office. I could hear voices inside. Aunt Shirley put her finger to her lips, and we both leaned in and put our ear to the door.

"You're being a little harsh, aren't you?" a male voice asked.

"Really, Daniel? You think you have a right to judge me?" I recognized Blair's voice.

My eyes widened when I realized we were overhearing Blair and Daniel fighting. Aunt Shirley gave me a knowing grin. We went back to listening.

"I know Samantha was up to something," Blair said. "Just like I know what you've done. You better fix this, or Samantha won't be the last dead body around here!"

I shook my head in amazement. Had I really just heard what I thought? Did Blair just admit to killing Samantha?

"Ahem."

I cringed at the sound behind me. I recognized the owner. I turned and saw Garrett glaring at me. "What are you two doing here?"

"Nothing," I squeaked.

His eyebrows shot up. "Nothing? Because it looked to me like you were eavesdropping on a private conversation."

"Nothing of the sort," Aunt Shirley said as she waved a hand in the air. "We were just about to knock on the door but didn't want to disturb the Watkinses if they were busy."

"Uh-huh. And did you hear anything interesting?"

I gulped, unsure how to answer. My brother, Matt, was standing next to Garrett in the narrow hallway, hands on his hips, shaking his head at me. I felt even worse.

"We couldn't hear a thing through this thick door," Aunt Shirley lied. "We don't even know who's inside."

"Sure," Garrett said. "Well, how about you two stand back and let us do our job."

"Are you here to arrest Daniel or Blair?" I blurted out.

"I have no official comment at this time," Garrett said. "But as soon as I do, I'll phone the paper and let you know."

I scowled at him. I hated it when he pulled that superior crap on me. "In that case, Aunt Shirley and I will stand back over here and just simply observe as citizens of this great city."

Garrett chuckled. "You do that."

Matt backed up and flattened himself against the wall next to Garrett to let Aunt Shirley and me pass. I gave Garrett one last glare as I walked by him, then let out a little squeal as I felt a gentle pat on my backside.

I whirled and glared at Garrett. He surreptitiously winked at me, and I couldn't help the grin that split my face.

I turned back around and started back down the hallway when I saw Lexi peek out of the room she was in. "What's going on?"

"I'm not really sure," I said. "But I think maybe Blair or Daniel is about to get arrested or something."

Lexi sucked in a breath. "Are you sure? How can this be?"

I shrugged. "I'm actually not sure of anything."

Lexi worked her lower lip between her teeth. "Should I call an attorney? This is horrible."

A few seconds later we heard yelling inside the office. Garrett and Matt emerged a few minutes later each carrying a laptop computer.

"I demand to know when we will get these back," Blair screeched at Garrett.

"Ma'am, this is a murder investigation. I believe I just explained to you that you and your husband are both suspects in this case. I don't have to answer any of your questions."

He and Matt walked out of the hallway and back into the store. I looked wide-eyed at Aunt Shirley. So they were looking at both computers. Did this have to do with the corporate espionage or the ledger of numbers that had been clutched in Samantha's hand?

Lexi pushed past me and ran down the hall to Blair and Daniel. "What's going on? Are you okay? Why does the police have your computers?"

Blair held up a hand to Lexi and then turned to glare at Daniel. "Everything had better be taken care of within the next day or two. Do you understand me?"

Daniel scowled at his wife. "This isn't over."

Blair snorted. "As far as I'm concerned it is. Fix this, then get your stuff out of our house."

Lexi's mouth fell open. "Blair, what's going on?"

Blair turned her flashing eyes on Lexi. "I can't do this right now. I need some privacy."

Blair stepped back and slammed the door in all of our faces. Daniel didn't say a word, just shoved his way through Aunt Shirley and me. I jumped back against the wall at the last minute to keep him from running us over.

The only people left in the hallway were Lexi, Aunt Shirley, and me. Aunt Shirley motioned us all into the room where Lexi had been working. This room was exactly set up like the others, with a desk, two love seats, and a platform for the bride to stand on while being measured.

Aunt Shirley led us to the love seats and sat down. "Lexi, would it be okay if Ryli and I asked you some questions?"

CHAPTER 10

Lexi's face registered surprise at Aunt Shirley's request. "Sure, I guess. I mean, I have no idea what's going on right now. Just because Samantha and I have been with the company the longest, doesn't mean any of us are close or anything."

"But you've been here the longest," Aunt Shirley argued. "You'd recognize certain signs even if you didn't understand them at the time."

Lexi frowned. "Like what?"

"Like behaviors," I supplied. "Have there been changes in anyone's behavior?"

Lexi pursed her lips in thought. "Yes. I think most of us are going through that. We are still relatively new in this community and in getting the store successfully launched. We've all been a little on edge lately because of the...well, let's just say there're some weird things happening around here."

"Like the customer complaints and the competition knowing ahead of time what's going to be on sale?" I asked. "That sort of thing?"

Lexi blinked in surprise. "How did you know all that?"

"Remember when I told you Samantha had contacted me to come to the store early yesterday?" I asked. "Well, it was about those very things. She thought she knew who was sabotaging the company and wanted my help."

"Sabotaging the company?" Lexi parroted. "What do you mean?"

"Do you know what corporate espionage is?" Aunt Shirley asked.

Lexi frowned. "I used to watch a TV show where the bad-guy-turned-good would go in and help capture people who were doing bad things in a company. Do you mean like that?"

Aunt Shirley nodded. "Yes. Corporate espionage is when a rival company hires a person within the competing company to spy for them. The rival company will give the spy a lot of money in exchange for information that could ultimately take down the competition."

"What does this have to do with Quilter's Paradise or why Samantha was killed?"

Aunt Shirley paused before answering. "Ryli and I believe that either Samantha was working for your competition in Kansas City, which is how they knew what was going to be on sale each week and why the company was having financial problems, and she was killed by someone who found out. Or she knew who was working for the competition and when she confronted him or her, Samantha was killed."

Lexi said nothing for a good thirty seconds. "Let me get this straight. If we go with the assumption that Samantha was this spy you talk about, and someone killed her because they found out...that someone would be a person that works here at Quilter's Paradise, right?"

I nodded. "I'd say that's about right."

"But the people that would be most affected would be Blair and Daniel. Are you saying either Blair or Daniel murdered

Samantha?" She stuck her thumbnail in her mouth and started to chew. "No. I can't see it. I know Blair seems high strung right now, but believe me, she's usually a very sweet, kind woman."

I schooled my face so I gave nothing away. But if I had a dime for every time I heard someone say that about someone who turned out to be evil, I could retire. "Okay, so if you don't think Blair could have done it. Do you think Daniel could?"

Lexi jerked back. "I don't know. These are terrible questions to think about. I can't answer—no, I don't *want* to answer them!"

"Not even if it helped catch a killer and brought justice to Samantha?" Aunt Shirley asked.

Lexi's face crumbled. "I guess I can try. Do I think Daniel could be angry enough to kill Samantha if he thought she was selling company secrets to a competitor and causing the store to go bankrupt?" She closed her eyes, and when she opened them, tears threatened to spill out. "Yes. I believe Daniel might be capable of it. But only recently."

"Why just recently?" Aunt Shirley asked.

Lexi chewed on her lower lip. "Blair is very tight lipped about her marriage, but she has confided in me recently that Daniel has been drinking pretty heavily, and I've noticed that sometimes he leaves for an extended period of time and no one knows where he's at...not even Blair."

I was dying to ask if she knew Samantha had been found clutching a ledger in her hand when she died, but I honestly didn't think she would be privy to that information yet.

"What about the other theory?" Aunt Shirley asked. "What if Samantha wanted to confront someone that she believed was hurting the company. Someone who may have suddenly come into money, or maybe someone who has been acting strange lately?"

Lexi frowned. "I really don't know anyone here. I live over in Brywood and drive to Granville every day. I don't know where any of the other employees live, so I wouldn't know if they've suddenly come into money. And as far as someone suddenly acting strange...again, just Daniel."

Not looking good for Daniel.

"I'm sorry I can't help anymore," Lexi said. "And I hope you don't think I'm being rude, but I really need to get the newsletters finalized and ready to go by tomorrow."

"Do you design the newsletters yourself?" I asked.

Lexi nodded. "Yes. I usually start out with a funny quote or some kind of inspirational affirmation at the top, and then I design the newsletter."

Aunt Shirley frowned. "The weekly sales and newsletter comes out on Thursdays. And that's what tells customers what will be on sale. Yet somehow the competition is getting advanced warning on this?"

Lexi nodded her head. "Yes. But I've never been able to figure out how that's possible. Only Blair, Samantha, and I know what the weekend sale items will be."

"Thank you, Lexi, for taking the time to talk with us," I said. "We'll leave you to your work."

"Thank you. I just hope Blair will open the door and talk with me soon. I'm overwhelmed at the possibility of doing all this on my own. I'm kind of taking on Samantha's responsibilities until we can hire another manager. I have my own responsibilities, and now with Blair and Daniel having problems, I'm trying to juggle their end, too." Lexi ran her fingers through her hair. "It's a tad bit overwhelming."

"I hope things get better for you," I said.

"Oh, one more thing," Aunt Shirley said. "Where were you last night?"

"Excuse me?" Lexi gritted out behind clenched teeth.

"It's an innocent question," Aunt Shirley said. "I'm assuming a police officer has already asked you where you were during the time of death. I was just wondering if you would share that information with us."

I swear I could physically see Lexi counting to ten to control her temper. "I was at home. I left the store around six-thirty. Blair and Samantha were still here working. The three of us have been putting in long hours getting the store up and running. I drove home to Brywood, and after a quick dinner, I started working on my next inspirational saying for this week's newsletter."

"So you were alone?" Aunt Shirley hounded.

"Yes. But I didn't kill Samantha. I worked on my newsletter then went to bed."

***

"I say we go by the Granville Hotel and see if the fiancé is still around," Aunt Shirley said as I fired up the Falcon. "I'd like to get his take on Samantha and whether or not he thinks she could be the spy."

"Do you really think he'll tell us if she was the spy or not?"

Aunt Shirley shrugged. "Worth a shot."

Five minutes later I pulled into a slot in front of the Granville Hotel. Aunt Shirley pulled open the ornate, gold-plated door of the hotel and we walked inside the dimly-lit foyer. The smell of mildew and stale smoke greeted me, and it was all I could do not to turn around and walk back out.

"How can I help you?" the older lady behind the counter rasped as we approached. I loathed to walk any closer. I could see a thin line of smoke curling upward toward her face from the counter.

I had no idea who she was…and that was saying a lot. I thought I knew just about everyone in Granville. Outside of the years in college, I'd lived in Granville my whole life. I placed her in between Mom and Aunt Shirley's age, with curly silver hair and a heavily-wrinkled, leathery face.

"You two needing a room?" she asked as she blew out three perfect smoke rings. She squinted her eyes at me, then looked over at Aunt Shirley. "This isn't no funny business, is it?" She pointed her cigarette hand at me. "This lady hasn't kidnapped you and is now selling you into some kind of kinky se—"

"No!" Aunt Shirley and I shouted at the same time.

The lady's bony shoulders shrugged. "Hey, you do what I do for as long as I have, you learn to start asking questions."

My heart plummeted at that thought. While I'm not totally naive to the goings on in the outside world, never would I have looked at someone like Aunt Shirley and me and instantly thought human trafficking. I looked past her into the room behind her and could see the soft glow of a TV.

"Are you the lady that bought the place a few years back?" I asked.

"Yep." She stubbed out the cigarette. "My name's Enid."

"Well, Enid, I can assure you my aunt and I are not here for anything nefarious, nor are we even here for a room for that matter."

Enid squinted her eyes at us. "Then why're you here?"

"We are hoping to talk with someone you have staying here," Aunt Shirley supplied.

"I can't tell you who's staying here."

"Could you at least get a message to him" I asked. "It's important we speak to him. It's about his fiancée who was recently killed."

Enid's eyes clouded with sympathy. "Oh, yes. Poor boy…and so polite."

I pulled out a business card and handed it to Enid. She took it then scowled. "You're with the newspaper? You want to hound this poor boy in his time of sorrow?"

"It's not like that," I said quickly. "I was one of the last people to see his fiancée, Samantha, before she was killed. I was hoping he could help answer a few questions I had after talking with Samantha."

Enid continued to scowl at us and then nodded her head once. "Fine. I will tell him."

"Thank you," I said. "We really appreciate it."

The minute we hit the outside, I inhaled the fresh air deep in my lungs, held it a couple seconds, then exhaled quickly. I repeated the process once more. Anything to get the nasty stale smoke smell out of my nostrils.

"I'm almost afraid to get inside the Falcon," I said. "I don't want the inside to reek."

"I'm still offended she thought I was a sex trafficker," Aunt Shirley huffed as she crossed her arms over her saggy chest. "The nerve!"

I chuckled. "Yeah, that was kinda funny. I mean, not the seriousness of what she was accusing us of, but the fact she immediately went there with you."

Aunt Shirley grunted. "If you say so."

"Where to now?" I asked, hoping to get her in a better mood.

"Let's grab some lunch and then go back to the paper. We need to get some addresses and talk with some employees."

CHAPTER 11

"I just got off the phone with Willa Trindle's mom," Aunt Shirley said. "She said Willa will be home around ten after five tonight and we could stop by then and chat."

Perfect!

I knew Aunt Shirley would be the best person to call and ask about coming over, seeing as how Mrs. Trindle and I never saw eye-to-eye on anything. She'd once told my mom she thought I was bad-mannered and wild growing up and adulthood hadn't improved me much. Obviously, Aunt Shirley was going to be our best bet on getting productive information from the Trindles...and it's not every day I can say something like that.

I snagged a lukewarm fry and munched on it while I went over questions and theories regarding the murder. Since I couldn't pin down whether or not Samantha was the spy or not, I knew my 'what-if' questions still had to be from a standpoint of playing both sides—what if she was the spy; what if she'd confronted the spy.

"Sinclair," Hank hollered from his office a little while later, "don't forget I need you to run over to the community theater and take some pictures of the upcoming play."

I groaned and glanced at my watch. I had completely forgotten. It was a little after three. If I left now I'd probably make it before they started for the day. Community play practice was from three-thirty to five-thirty Monday through Friday. It never changed.

I got Aunt Shirley's attention and we made our way to the Chapman Theater off of Main Street. Gracie Chapman had been a prestigious and wealthy old lady who lived in Granville years ago. She had a well-known love for the arts and music. When she died, she left a lot of money to the city to be specifically used to support local arts programs. When the high school drama teacher Mrs. Drago retired, she decided to take up the torch and start a community theater program. It was a successful endeavor and Granville citizens of all ages tried out for the two plays a year the theater put on.

I yanked open the ornate handle of the old brick building and strolled inside. I could hear voices coming from inside the auditorium. Aunt Shirley and I quietly walked through a doorway that led us to the stage.

The Chapman Theater had originally started out as a nickelodeon way back in the day. When the movie theater closed down in the sixties, the screen was torn down and a stage erected. The auditorium could comfortably seat a hundred people downstairs and at least thirty people in the balcony upstairs.

I saw Mrs. Drago talking to a group of people in front of the stage. She hadn't changed much from when I had her as a teacher in school. Pencil skirt, sensible blouse and shoes, and her silver hair pulled into a bun. I waited until she'd finished talking before tapping her on the shoulder.

"Hello, Mrs. Drago."

Mrs. Drago smiled and gave me a one-arm hug. "Ryli Sinclair. I'm so glad you could make it today. I wasn't sure you'd find the time, what with—well, you know, the murder and all. I didn't know if you would be busy with that."

"Never too busy for you and your theater," I assured her. "I was hoping if everyone was here, I could get a couple pictures for the paper."

"I think I still have a couple people not here, but they should arrive shortly. I don't believe I know your partner."

I introduced Mrs. Drago to Aunt Shirley. "I was Ryli's drama teacher in high school."

"I didn't know you were in plays," Aunt Shirley said.

"Sometimes," I snorted.

Mrs. Drago gave me a sympathetic look. "Ryli had her own drama with another student. Speaking of, I hear she's working at the store where the murder took place."

I nodded. "Yep. In fact, we are heading to Willa's house after we finish up here. I have a few questions I want to ask."

Mrs. Drago chuckled and gave me a knowing look. "Under the guise of journalistic information, right?"

I grinned and lifted an eyebrow. "Of course."

"Did that girl ever give you a moment's peace?" Aunt Shirley asked.

"No. Not until I moved away and went to college."

Mrs. Drago patted my arm. "And look how far you've come. Just be careful when you talk with her today. I don't know if she's a suspect or not, but it's no secret how jealous she is of you."

"She's a suspect as far as I am concerned," Aunt Shirley said. "But you don't need to worry, I got Ryli's back. I obviously don't know the whole story between Willa and Ryli, but Willa won't get by with anything when I'm around."

My chest swelled with gratitude for Aunt Shirley. I've learned over the year that Aunt Shirley was definitely someone you want in your corner. We've had more close calls than I care to count, but every time she was there fighting by my side.

A few minutes later everyone had finally arrived and I was able to get a few pictures for the newspaper. With another promise to be careful with my investigation of the murder, Aunt Shirley and I went back to the office so I could write up a blurb about the play for the paper. While I typed up the article, Mindy looked up Ronni Reynolds's address. I figured we'd swing by her house after we visited with Willa.

By the time I finished the article and sent it to Hank, it was a little after five. My stomach did a little flip at the thought of what Aunt Shirley and I were about to do—enter the enemy's camp. But I needed some answers as far as Samantha's murder went, so I was willing to do what needed to be done.

Aunt Shirley and I said good night to Mindy as we grabbed our purses and left the office. I fired up the Falcon and headed to Willa's place over on Cherry Street. I drove slow enough that we wouldn't be too early.

Willa still lived with her mother. Her dad had split when Willa was in the fifth grade. She barely had a chance with a mom like hers…when her dad left, Willa went to hell in a handbasket. She became a mean girl. I was actually relieved when I moved away to go to college. It meant I could finally be free to do whatever I wanted without having to constantly look over my shoulder.

Aunt Shirley and I hadn't even made it halfway up the front walkway before the door was pulled open. Mrs. Trindle stood in the doorway, her arms folded over her chest, feet spread apart, and an imposing look on her face.

"You're late."

My footsteps faltered. I wasn't late, but I wasn't quite sure how to say that without offending her. I needed her and her daughter to open up to me. If they had anything to do with Samantha's murder, nothing would give me more pleasure than to be the one to ferret the information out.

"We ain't late," Aunt Shirley countered. "We were just giving your daughter time to get home and relax before we asked her some questions."

Mrs. Trindle gave a slow nod. "Fine. Come in. My Willa is in the kitchen having dinner. It's very important for her to constantly eat so she keeps up her energy. She's one of those unfortunate souls who can never seem to eat enough. She tries so hard to gain weight, but she always remains so thin and—oh, I'm sorry, Ryli. I forget not everyone is cursed with needing to gain weight. You'll want to keep a watchful eye on that before you get married."

I jerked back as though I'd been struck. I actually had to rerun her last sentence through my brain to make sure she said what I thought she said. I looked over at Aunt Shirley. Her nostrils were flared and her mouth was pinched. She caught the caddy statement, too.

"We won't keep her," I said. I suddenly hoped with all my heart I could pin this murder on Willa. She and her mom needed knocked off their pedestals.

Willa was sitting at a round, four-person table in the middle of the kitchen, picking at her dinner. When she saw us walk into the room, she quickly set her fork down.

"Ryli, I'm glad you could swing by. It's been ages since we got together like this."

She and I both knew we'd never gotten together like this. "I really just needed to ask you a few questions. If you don't mind."

Willa spread her arms wide. "Of course not. I have nothing to hide, obviously."

We'll see about that.

Mrs. Trindle grabbed Willa's glass and proceeded to fill her cup with some regular cola. "Ryli, I have some diet if you'd like a drink."

I gritted my teeth. "No thank you. Aunt Shirley and I just finished having a bite to eat at the Burger Barn," I lied.

Mrs. Trindle tsked and waggled a finger at me. "You be careful. Keep that up and you won't be able to fit into your wedding dress."

The only thing that kept me from leaping over the table and going all spider monkey on her was the fact I could tell Aunt Shirley was wanting to do the same thing. Someone needed to have a clear head. I let the snide comment slide once again.

"We won't take up too much of your time, Willa," I assured her. "Like I said, I just want to ask you a couple questions about the murder."

Willa looked me over shrewdly. "Is this going in the paper? Will my name be in the paper?"

I knew what she wanted to hear. "Front page story."

Willa's face lit up. "In that case, ask whatever you want."

I surreptitiously glanced at Aunt Shirley. She nodded her head. Just that small encouragement help bolster my courage. "When was the last time you saw the victim, Samantha?"

Willa looked up toward the ceiling. "Let's see. I guess Tuesday evening. That was the day you came into the store for your wedding veil fitting, correct?"

I nodded. "Yes."

"Well, I closed that night. Sometimes I open the store, and sometimes I close the store. My schedule as far as hours varies. However, I'm lucky enough to have Monday's off, which gives me a two-day weekend."

"Samantha closed as well that night?" Aunt Shirley asked.

"Yes. What does this have to do with an article for the paper?" Willa demanded impatiently. "These are the type of questions your *boyfriend* asked me."

I decided to change my course of questions. If there was one thing Willa loved, it was gossip. "Do you like working for Quilter's Paradise? They seem to be doing a great business."

Willa nodded. "It's a great company! We do a lot of business and generate a lot of sales, even though I've been hearing lately that things are on a downward spiral."

I pretended to be surprised. "Really? What's going on?"

Willa sat forward in her chair. "Well, from what I've been able to piece together, someone is leaking information to a competing store in Kansas City on what our sale items are going to be for the big weekend business."

"Wow," I said. "Any idea who it is?"

Willa snickered. "Obviously it was Samantha. I'd say either Blair or Daniel found out and they killed her."

I blinked in surprise. Willa said it with so much matter-of-factness I couldn't believe it. "You honestly think Blair or Daniel killed Samantha?"

"Duh. Who else could it be?"

I said nothing, but went with another tactic. "Have you noticed anyone lately who has come into some money?" As I asked the question, I looked around Willa's kitchen. All the appliances were old, but that didn't mean anything definite.

"Maybe," Willa shrugged. "Ronni Reynolds has a new ride, why?"

"No reason. Now that Samantha's position is open, do you think there will be a lot of interest in her role as manager?"

Mrs. Trindle had been silent up to this point. "If anyone deserves that position, it's my Willa. She works so hard up there at that store, slaving away eight hours a day, five days a week. And do they appreciate her? No! She hasn't had a raise in over two months!"

"Yeah," Willow added, "and when I do have to call in sick, Samantha or Lexi really ride me hard. I can't help it I have frequent headaches and have to call in sick a lot."

"If they know what's good for them," Mrs. Trindle said, "they will promote my Willa to manager."

Nothing creepy about that statement.

"Am I sorry Samantha died?" Willa asked. "Yes. But someone needs to step up to the plate. And I'm that someone. From what I hear, Samantha was doing a crappy job." She smiled ominously at her mom. "I even heard there were numerous online complaints about how she was running things."

"My Willa will know how to run that store when she gets the manager's position."

Willa looked at her watch. "I really need to wrap this up. I have plans tonight."

"Of course." I turned to Aunt Shirley. "Do you have anything to ask?"

"Seems you asked all the important questions. We don't want to keep you."

Willa tossed her blond hair over one of her shoulders. "I have a date tonight with Tristan Rainer."

I blinked in surprise. "Tristan? He's back in Granville?"

Willa gave an obvious surprised gasp and covered her mouth. "Oh, that's right. Didn't you two date in high school?"

Tristan Rainer had been the captain of the football team and all-around super jock. We did not date in high school. And Willa darn well knew it. I had a mad crush on him, but he never knew I existed…especially when Willa did everything she could to snag him.

"We didn't date," I gritted out.

"Well, if we keep dating, you wouldn't mind if I bring him to your wedding in October, would you?"

Over my dead body will either one of you be at my wedding!

CHAPTER 12

"What do you think?" I asked Aunt Shirley as we settled into the front seat of the Falcon.

Aunt Shirley blew out a breath. "I think if Willa didn't do it, her mother might have. I had no idea that woman was so crazy."

I laughed humorlessly. "I did. You should hear the things she says about me. And then for Willa to instantly grab onto Tristan the minute he comes back to town and want to parade him in front of me...makes me so mad! I'm not jealous or anything. I mean, please, I have Garrett. There's no comparison. But the constant needling me for an invite and assuming she's coming to my wedding is getting old."

"I understand. But I'm not sure that makes her a murderer."

"I know. I just wanted to say it out loud."

Aunt Shirley snorted. "Believe it or not, I totally understand. I had my fair share of petty girlfriends in my time. We aren't that different, my dear."

"Bite your tongue."

Aunt Shirley chuckled. "I say we go find Ronni Reynolds' house and—"

My cell phone rang, cutting Aunt Shirley off.

"Hello?"

I gave Aunt Shirley a thumbs-up when the caller said he was Samantha's fiancé and he would like to meet up with me and talk.

He gave me his room number, and I hung up with the promise I'd see him in five minutes.

"Let's swing by Burger Barn and grab some dinner," Aunt Shirley said. "I bet the boy hasn't eaten anything, and I sure could use some food."

We grabbed a couple cheeseburgers then headed to the Granville Hotel. We were a few minutes late, but I didn't think Samantha's fiancé would mind once he got a whiff of the food. Especially if his room smelled as bad as the hotel lobby.

We waved to Enid then walked down the narrow corridor until we found the room number. Aunt Shirley gave two soft raps on the door.

A thin, dark-haired man in his thirties opened the door. His eyes were bloodshot and his clothes looked like they'd been slept in.

"Hi," he croaked. "My name is Clifford Broman, but everyone calls me Cliff." He stepped back and we entered the dark room.

I was right. It didn't smell much better inside the room than it did in the lobby. I had to wonder if the beige walls weren't once white but now stained with smoke. There was a queen-sized bed in the middle of the room, a nightstand and small dresser, and a two-person table shoved in a corner. The bathroom was immediately to my left.

"My name is Ryli Sinclair and this is Aunt Shirley." I held up the bag. "We brought dinner if that's okay?"

One corner of Cliff's mouth lifted. "It's very kind of you. I don't know if I'll be able to eat much." He frowned. "In fact, I'm not sure if I've eaten anything since I found out about—"

96

Cliff put his head in his hands and started to weep. I looked wide-eyed at Aunt Shirley. I wasn't used to this kind of display by a man. I wanted to reach out and pat his shoulder but it seemed so trite.

"Here now," Aunt Shirley said as she pushed me aside and patted Cliff on the arm. "You come sit here at the table and Ryli will get our food."

I followed them to the tiny table and began pulling the food out of the bag and setting it on the table. Aunt Shirley dug into her purse and handed Cliff a miniature package of tissue. He thanked her and blew his nose.

Once the food was set out, I grabbed my cheeseburger and fries and sat down on the edge of the bed since there were no other chairs to sit in. I tucked my feet in under me and began to nibble on the cheeseburger. Cliff took a small bite and woodenly chewed the meat.

"Better?" Aunt Shirley asked.

He nodded. "Yes, thank you." He swallowed then set the cheeseburger back on the paper wrapping. Cliff turned his head to me. "So you were one of the last people to see my Samantha alive?"

My heart dipped at his use of "my Samantha."

"Yes. Aunt Shirley and I both were. Samantha helped me design a—" I broke off. I didn't want to mention anything about a wedding. "She helped me that morning at the store. It was then we first became aware that there might be a problem at the store."

Cliff nodded and picked up a fry. He stared at the fry for a few seconds before shoving it into his mouth. "I knew something was going on at her workplace. She wouldn't tell me what exactly, no matter how many times I pressed her. But last week, she finally caved, and then we had an awful fight about the store."

"About what?" Aunt Shirley asked.

Cliff sighed. "I'm the store manager for the competing company in Kansas City that is supposedly usurping Quilter's Paradise on the sale items."

My mouth dropped. Of all the things he could have said, that was a surprise. "Do you know how your company is getting the information?"

"I honestly don't." Cliff laughed humorlessly. "Samantha had even gone so far as to accuse me of listening to her talk in her sleep! I was so angry and hurt. But now I realized I should have paid more attention to what she was saying. Maybe if I had, she wouldn't be dead."

Aunt Shirley placed her hand on Cliff's. "Don't do that to yourself, son. None of us knew how serious this was. When we saw Samantha again Tuesday afternoon getting lunch, that's when she asked Ryli and me to stop by so she could talk with us."

Cliff frowned as he looked at me then Aunt Shirley. "No offense, but why did she want to talk to you about what was going on? I've never heard your names before or seen you over at the house in Kansas City, so it's not like you guys were friends."

"You're right," Aunt Shirley said. "Let's just say that Ryli and I have certain skills that come in handy when it comes to finding out information. Like investigators."

I barely refrained from rolling my eyes. "We work for the newspaper, so we are apt at digging up information."

And dead bodies.

98

Cliff took another bite of his cheeseburger, chewed, and swallowed. "I told Chief Kimble last night that I thought either Blair or Lexi killed Samantha."

Lexi?

"Why Lexi?" I asked.

Cliff snagged a fry and ate more heartedly. "I don't know. I guess because she's been with the company the longest, as long as Samantha. Lexi came over from the Columbia store just like Samantha, and she was riding Samantha so hard because of people leaving negative feedback on the website."

"That seems like a huge leap to murder," I argued.

Anger flashed in Cliff's eyes. "What do you want me to say? I have no idea who would do this to my fiancée. She was a wonderful person. I can't imagine anyone doing to her what they did!"

"What if I told you," Aunt Shirley said looking at Cliff shrewdly, "that a lot of people think that Samantha was a spy for the company you work for."

Cliff banged his hand on the table. "Then I'd tell you they were a bunch of liars. Samantha wasn't a spy. She took her job very seriously. So much so, when she first found out where I worked, she almost didn't date me."

"How did you meet Samantha?" I asked.

Cliff closed his eyes as though lost in a memory. "Her old college roommate married a friend of mine. We met at their wedding and hit it off."

"You mentioned you thought Lexi might have killed Samantha for reasons you don't know," I said. "Why would you suspect Blair, also?"

Cliff took one more bite of his cheeseburger then crumpled up the last of the uneaten food and tossed it in the bag. "Blair is easier to explain. Blair used to be warm, friendly, and just an all-around kind person. That's why Samantha agreed to help her open the Granville store. Well, that and the fact we would actually be closer than when she lived in Columbia. But from what Samantha has said recently, Blair has changed. She's become angrier, she lashes out at her employees, and it's no secret the store is having problems."

"But that doesn't explain why she'd kill Samantha," I said.

"Tuesday night, before Samantha was going to leave the store for the night, she called me on her cell. She said Blair was in a rage about the store receiving so much negativity lately and that she was blaming Samantha for it."

"So you believe," Aunt Shirley surmised, "Blair became so enraged over the reputation and potential loss of income from the store that she killed Samantha?"

Cliff shrugged. "It makes the most sense."

I cocked my head and arched an eyebrow at Aunt Shirley. I had to agree...it did make the most sense. And didn't Lexi tell us when she left the store the night Samantha was killed, both Blair and Samantha were still there?

"Thank you so much for talking with us," Aunt Shirley said and rose from the table. "If you remember anything, or just need us for any reason, please feel free to call on us."

Cliff stood up from the table and extended his hand to each of us. "Thank you so much for stopping by. I actually feel better than I have since I first found out what happened."

"One last thing," I asked. "Have you tried calling Samantha's cell phone? It seems to have went missing."

"I know. The Chief guy asked me if Samantha had a phone and I told him yes. She went everywhere with it. I have no idea where it could be."

Cliff led us to the door and saw us out. We waved again to Enid as we crossed the lobby and made our way outside. The sun was still high in the sky, even though it was going on six o'clock.

"Want to make a run by Ronni's house before I drop you off at the Manor?" I asked.

"You know it." Aunt Shirley retrieved the paper Mindy had given us with Ronni's address on it. I wasn't exactly sure of the house, but I knew the street.

A few minutes later I pulled the Falcon onto Maplewood Drive. On this side of town, the houses were fairly new with huge oak trees in every yard. We found Ronni's house and parked two houses down from her house.

Aunt Shirley whistled. "Notice the company sign in the yard? They are adding on to the back of the house and fixing the roof."

"Yes, but that doesn't mean anything."

Aunt Shirley sent me a look. "She also has a brand new 2017 Charger sitting in her drive. That's a pretty nice car for someone who works at a quilt shop."

I had to admit, it didn't look good for Ronni. "But what is her motive?"

"If your new sister-in-law wasn't knocked up, I'd say call her and we'd have a girls' night in, drink margaritas, and pouring over suspects and motives."

I chuckled. "Let me call her. She may want to get out of the house, even though she can't drink."

"You do that," Aunt Shirley said. "Meanwhile, I think we should go knock on the door and see what's up with Ronni."

No sooner had the words left Aunt Shirley's mouth than Ronni's front door opened. A slender woman with dark, spikey hair sauntered out and got in the brand-new car. Aunt Shirley and I ducked down low in the Falcon's seats as she drove past us.

"Looks like we'll need to confront her tomorrow," Aunt Shirley said. "Call Paige. Have her meet us at your place in twenty minutes."

CHAPTER 13

I plunked a bottle of hard creamsicle soda in front of Aunt Shirley. She wrinkled her nose. "What is this crap?"

"It's something new. It's a creamsicle but with booze," I said. "Just try it."

She slid the bottle across the table away from her. "I'm not drinking no sissy drink."

"Just try it," I insisted.

"Fine." Aunt Shirley twisted off the top and took a swig. Her eyes widened and she smacked her lips together as she read the bottle. "Yum. I bet I could drink like eight of these and be okay!"

I snorted. "How about you drink that one and we'll call it good."

Aunt Shirley gave me the evil eye. "How about you remember I'm a big girl and can drink whatever I want."

"It's a good thing Matt is working the night shift tonight," Paige said changing the subject as she poured herself a glass of cucumber-infused water from the pitcher on the table. "This way I don't have to explain what I am doing tonight."

"Same for me with Garrett." I poured myself a glass of the cucumber-infused water and sat back in the chair.

Aunt Shirley scoffed at us. "You two worry too much about what your men think."

I stared her down. "And you don't worry enough about what Old Man Jenkins thinks. Aren't you afraid one day he's going to get tired of chasing you and move on to someone else who will be less challenging?"

"Nope." Aunt Shirley shoved a notebook and pen at Paige. "You take notes while Ryli and I go over what we know so far."

"Let's start at the top and work down," I said, taking the hint that Aunt Shirley didn't want to talk about Old Man Jenkins. "We have Blair, Daniel, Cliff, Lexi, Willa, and Ronni."

Paige's mouth dropped open. "Willa Trindle? As in your arch-nemesis? She's a suspect?"

"Yep." I grinned mischievously at Paige and took a sip of water.

"Let's start with Blair Watkins," Aunt Shirley said and Paige scribbled the name on the paper. "Motive to kill Samantha might be because she found out Samantha was a spy for a competing company and was causing Quilter's Paradise to nearly go bankrupt. So Blair killed Samantha out of anger."

As Paige scrambled to keep up, I thought about Daniel. "Daniel's reason to kill Samantha might be because Samantha found out Daniel was taking money from the company or somehow manipulating the books. Hence the paper she was clutching in her hands when she was found."

Aunt Shirley frowned. "I still can't believe he wouldn't have taken that from her after he killed her."

"Maybe he didn't see she had it," Paige suggested.

I was with Aunt Shirley on this one…it did seem odd that Daniel would leave behind such a damaging clue.

"Now," Aunt Shirley continued, "the fiancé, Cliff, is a little harder to pin down for motive."

Paige gasped. "She was engaged? And you guys suspect her fiancé? That's horrible."

"In a murder investigation," Aunt Shirley grumbled, "everyone is a suspect. Now, back to Cliff. He's admitted to being the manager of the company that is somehow getting secret information from Quilter's Paradise. It makes the most sense to assume he not only knew Samantha was spying for his company, but that she was giving him the information she gleaned."

"Why kill her?" I asked.

Aunt Shirley frowned. "Maybe Samantha suspected Blair was on to her. Maybe she told Cliff she wouldn't spy anymore and in a fit of rage he killed her. Does it in her workplace to throw suspicion around."

I shrugged. "I actually like that theory."

Paige gasped. "You *like* that theory?"

I chuckled. "I mean I'm okay with that theory. Of course I don't want it to be the fiancé."

I only said that last part because I knew what a romantic Paige was. It would kill her if she thought a woman was killed by the man she loved. I've been through enough murders the last year to know people kill for all kinds of selfish reasons.

"Next on the list is Lexi," Paige said. "What's her motive?"

"I'm not sure," Aunt Shirley admitted. "Blair, Lexi, and Samantha pretty much run the company together. But, Lexi is privy to sensitive information like what goes on sale each week. Maybe Lexi is the spy and Samantha found out and Lexi killed her."

"I can get behind that," I said. "Except she's constantly blowing a gasket over how poorly the store is doing. She was harassing Samantha about the negative feedback. Why would she care how the store is doing if she was trying to sabotage the store?"

"To throw suspicion?" Paige suggested.

Aunt Shirley snorted. "We have a lot of suspicion being thrown around it seems. We have nothing concrete or solid."

"Let's move on to Willa," I said. "I can give you a thousand reasons why she'd kill someone. The fact she's unbalanced is one."

Paige snickered. "I've been doing this with you guys long enough now to know that's not gonna fly as a motive."

I shrugged and hid my smile behind my glass of water. "No. But it's true."

"Get focused," Aunt Shirley scowled. "Willa's motive is obvious. She wanted Samantha's job and she made no bones about it. Greed is a powerful motive to kill. She was outside the sub shop the day we all spoke, so she knew Samantha was wanting to talk with us. Plus, I don't like the strange way her and her mom have already determined Willa will get Samantha's old job. It's very suspicious if you ask me."

Paige leaned over the paper and scribbled down Willa's motive. "Okay. Last on the list is Ronni? What's her motive?"

"This one is also easy," I said. "She's driving an expensive, brand-new car, her house is getting remodeled, she's living high on the hog on a cashier's salary? I don't think so. I'd say of all our suspects, Ronni is the spy and she's blatantly using the money she gets from the company."

"And you think Samantha figured out it was Ronni, she called Ronni back to the store later that night to confront her, and then Ronni killed her?" Paige asked.

I looked at Aunt Shirley. "Makes the most sense to me out of everything we've laid out."

Aunt Shirley nodded. "It does. What bothers me is the paper Samantha was clutching. What would that have to do with Ronni?"

"I don't know," I admitted. "But at least we have all the players accounted for. And I'd say after hashing it out amongst us, Ronni is our main suspect."

Aunt Shirley took a long swig of her drink and wiped her mouth with the back of her hand. "Agreed."

"I say we go to the store around ten and see if we can't talk with Ronni more in depth," I said.

Paige glanced at her watch. "I better head back home. Matt gets off in about an hour, and I still have no idea what I'm fixing for dinner. These late work nights are murder. I'm usually feeding my cravings from seven until eight when he gets home. I'm going to gain over a hundred pounds with this pregnancy at this rate."

She got up from her chair and looked at me sheepishly. "I better use your bathroom before I leave." She rubbed her swollen belly then took off down the hallway.

"I can just have Paige take me to the Manor tonight so you don't have to get out," Aunt Shirley offered.

"That would be great. I'll pick you up around eight for the office."

Paige came back and the two of them left soon after. I decided to text Garrett and see if he was going to drop by before heading to his house for the night. A few minutes later he responded saying he'd be at my house around eight, but not to worry he'd already eaten. Which was a good thing considering the only thing I had to eat was soup or cereal.

Since I had about an hour to spare, I decided to run a bubble bath and relax. I still wasn't convinced that Daniel or Blair wasn't involved with Samantha's murder. I hoped some quiet alone time might help me think.

I poured Garrett's favorite scent, vanilla lavender, into the tub and poured a glass of pinot noir as I waited for the tub to fill. A few minutes later, I pulled up the latest audiobook I was listening to and sank into the warm water.

I'd been listening for about ten minutes when the reader was interrupted by the ringing of my cell phone. I quickly wiped my hand on a nearby towel and swiped to answer the phone.

"Hello?"

No one answered.

"Hello?"

When I still didn't get a response, I pulled the phone away from my ear and looked at the number. It wasn't a number my phone recognized. Nor did I recognize the area code. I put the phone back up to my ear.

"Is anyone there?"

Silence.

I hung up and the audiobook picked back up again. I grabbed my wine glass and took a drink before standing up and drying off. I wrapped a towel around me and headed into my bedroom to get dressed. I threw the phone down on the bed, still listening to my book.

Once again the reader's voice was cut off and my cell phone rang through. It was the same number that called a few minutes earlier. I now recognized the five-seven-three area code. A little more than peeved, I swiped open the phone and all but screamed a hello. Enough was enough.

Silence.

"What do you want? You realize all I have to do is call this number back, right?"

Silence.

"My fiancé is the chief of police. All he has to do is trace this number and you'll be in trouble."

At first I thought the caller was softly panting...but then I realized they were softly laughing.

The caller hung up.

The spit in my mouth dried up, and I could feel myself shaking. I grabbed a pair of yoga pants and a t-shirt from my closet and threw them on. With trembling hands I pulled my hair back into a ponytail and hightailed it out to the living room. I double-checked the door to make sure it was locked.

I dashed back down the hall and grabbed my wine glass and phone. I knew I couldn't come right out and tell Garrett about the phone calls because he'd accuse me of sticking my nose in where it didn't belong...and if the phone belonged to the killer...he'd be right!

I heard a key being inserted in my front door. Taking two deep breaths I steadied my nerves and walked out to meet Garrett.

"You look all fresh and clean." He grabbed me around my waist and buried his nose in my neck. "And you smell good enough to eat."

I giggled in spite of the backflips happening in my stomach. "Thank you. I know how much you like this scent."

He leaned up and captured my lips and I lost myself in the moment. I willed myself to shut out the terror I was feeling and enjoy the feel of the man who was about to be my husband.

"Mmm…what's this all about?" Garrett whispered.

I smiled. "Just missed you today."

"Uh-huh." He leaned back and watched my face closely. "Is that all?"

"Yes. Gosh, can't I just miss you?"

Garrett flashed me a grin. "You bet." He kissed me again quickly on the lips. "I can't stay long. I have to be up early in the morning and I'm beat."

"You could stay here," I offered. I hoped he didn't catch the hopefulness in my voice.

He groaned then winked at me. "I would, but if I stay here we won't be going to bed at an early hour."

I wanted more than anything to tell him that was okay, but I knew it wouldn't be fair to him.

"Hey, did you happen to find Samantha's cell phone?" I asked nonchalantly.

Garrett's forehead furrowed. "No. I figure the killer took it."

Oh great.

"I don't suppose you happen to know the number?" I asked.

"What's this about?"

"Nothing! I just wondered if you knew the number."

He leaned down and picked up Miss Molly. She'd wound herself around his legs and was purring loudly. "I have the number at the office. It's not a number from around here. The area code was from Columbia. It was a five-seven-three number, I believe."

My heart plummeted to my stomach. It took all my effort not to throw up and then launch myself at Garrett and beg him to stay.

He set Miss Molly down and drew me back in his arms. "I really need to go." He ran one hand over my cheek. "Sweet dreams."

He kissed me once more and walked out the front door. "Don't forget to lock the door. I don't want anything happening to you."

Bite your tongue!

"Of course," I said. "Talk to you tomorrow."

I locked the bottom lock and the deadbolt and then leaned back against the door. I knew it would be a long night. I wouldn't be sleeping soundly.

I finished off my wine and gathered Miss Molly up in my arms and headed to my bedroom. It was still early, but I knew I'd need all the rest I could get.

"I love you so much, Miss Molly," I whispered into her fur. "But sometimes I wish you were a fierce guard dog."

CHAPTER 14

"You look like dog poop," Aunt Shirley said as she got in the Falcon. "Did that man of yours come over and keep you up all night?"

I laughed at the naughty gleam in her eye. I'd texted her earlier and told her I'd be about a half an hour late, but I didn't elaborate why.

"No. I had two phone calls from a Columbia area code last night. The caller didn't say anything, just laughed softly." I turned to look at Aunt Shirley. "I think it was Samantha's cell phone. Which means it was her killer."

"What?" Aunt Shirley sat up straight in her seat. "Did you tell Garrett?"

"No. He was exhausted and I didn't want to tell him why I wanted him to spend the night. So I tossed and turned the whole night. Scared out of my mind."

Aunt Shirley clucked her tongue. "You should have called. I'd have spent the night with you."

My heart lifted and I patted Aunt Shirley's hand. "Thanks. I think I finally fell asleep around three this morning."

"Well, you better start guzzling a load of coffee, because we got us a full day ahead."

I knew she was right, so I stopped off at a gas station and bought a coffeeccino—half coffee, half cappuccino mixture. The only thing the newspaper office would have brewing was Mindy's herbal teas. And they were usually caffeine free.

Aunt Shirley and I strolled through the doors of the *Granville Gazette* around eighty forty-five and waved to Mindy. Today she was dressed in white Capri pants with a midnight blue cut-out-shoulder top. Her teased hair was almost as high as her designer high heels.

"Morning you two." Mindy took a closer look at me. "Oh, Ryli, you look awful this morning."

I flinched. Obviously I was going to have to do something about my appearance before I went into public today.

"I don't mean to sound callous," Mindy said and motioned me over with her hand. "Come. Let me help you out."

I wheeled my chair, caffeinated drink in hand, over to where she was sitting. She reached into her top drawer and took out a miniature duffel bag full of makeup.

"So what's on your agenda today?" Mindy asked as she tilted my head upward. She grabbed a tube, squeezed out the contents, and applied it underneath my eyes.

"We're gonna go over to Quilter's Paradise and talk to Ronni," Aunt Shirley said. "Outside of either Blair or Daniel, she looks to be the main suspect."

"Sounds like you girls are coming along just fine." Mindy leaned back in her chair and surveyed me. "Much better."

"Actually," Aunt Shirley said, "that's a huge improvement."

I scowled at her as I grabbed the hand-held mirror Mindy offered me.

Wow! That is *a huge improvement.*

"Could you do my makeup for the wedding?" I asked Mindy.

Tears gathered in Mindy's eyes. "I'd love to do your makeup! Oh, this will be so much fun. Do you know what colors you want?"

"Ahem!" We all turned to stare at Hank. He was leaning against the doorframe of his office with a scowl on his face. He yanked out his unlit cigar. "I'm not sure why we're out here all giddy about makeup and colors when I have a paper that's coming out in a few days with no front-page story about a murder getting solved!"

Mindy smiled and waved her hand at Hank. "Oh, Hank. We're just talking about the wedding. And Ryli already told me they're inches from solving the case."

Hank eyed me. "This true?"

I opened my mouth to reply, but Aunt Shirley beat me to it. "Yes, it's true. Now go back inside your office, you old goat, and leave us to our work."

Hank snorted and pushed himself off the doorframe. "By the way, Ryli, how're those self-defense moves coming?"

I stifled a groan. I hadn't practiced at all. "They're coming. You'll see a huge improvement at our next meeting."

I heard Aunt Shirley let out a snort behind me, but I ignored her. I was too busy staring Hank down. He suddenly grinned and I felt my palms start to sweat.

"Good. We're gonna learn how to kick a weapon out of an assailant's hand next time. You can help me demonstrate to the class again." He turned and slammed the door to his office.

"Darn him!" I growled.

Aunt Shirley chuckled. "It's your fault for lying. He just called you on it." Aunt Shirley stood up. "Let's get. The store's been open for about fifteen minutes already."

"Keep me posted," Mindy hollered as we hurried out the door.

The parking lot at Quilter's Paradise was still relatively empty. I pulled the Falcon into a vacant spot near the front of the store and parked.

"I think we should see if we can't get a feel for Daniel if he's here," Aunt Shirley said. "Something about him I don't trust."

Willa was working the cash register. I felt the need to wave when she saw us walk in. She gave me a smile that didn't quite reach her eyes.

"Let's go to the back and see if we can find Ronni or Daniel," Aunt Shirley said.

We found Ronni in Aisle 2 stocking fabrics.

"Hello, Ronni," I said. "My name is Ryli Sinclair, and I'm a reporter with the *Granville Gazette*."

"Hello." Ronni turned and smiled at us. "Can I help you find something?"

"Actually, Ronni," I said, "we were hoping we could maybe set up a time tonight to talk with you."

Ronni frowned. "About what? The murder? I really don't want to talk to the paper just yet about what happened to Samantha. I hope you understand."

Aunt Shirley stepped forward and laid her hand on Ronni's arm. "We won't ask difficult questions. And we'll only take maybe ten or fifteen minutes."

Ronni looked anxiously down the aisle. "Okay. I get off around five. Can you come over to my house after that?"

My heart leaped. She was going to let us in to see all the money she was spending in renovations! "Sure."

"Do you know where I live?" Ronni asked.

I didn't want to say yes, we'd already spied on her once. "No."

Ronni gave me her address and Aunt Shirley and I continued to the back of the store to see if we could find Daniel. I wasn't exactly sure what we were going to say or how we were going to get him to talk with us.

A sudden commotion at the front of the store had Aunt Shirley and me peering to see what was going on.

"It's Garrett and Matt!" I exclaimed. "We need to hide!"

Aunt Shirley shot me an incredulous look. "Why?"

"Because they'll know we are up to something if they find us here!"

Aunt Shirley chuckled. "This is a girlie shop where you are getting your wedding veil. Why wouldn't you come in here?"

I knew Garrett would never buy that I was just in here shopping for the wedding. Unfortunately, I didn't have time to hide. His eyes locked with mine and I groaned aloud.

He strode down the back of the aisle where I was standing with Aunt Shirley. My knees started to shake.

"I like this one." Aunt Shirley shoved a plastic bundle of flowers in my arms. "Oh, and these. These are really nice." She shoved another plastic bundle at me. I had no recourse but to clutch onto them like they were a lifeline.

Garrett and Matt stopped in front of us. Both men had their arms crossed over their chests and scowls on their faces.

"What're you doing here?" Garrett asked.

He was looking at me, but Aunt Shirley answered. "We're picking out flowers for the wedding," she snapped. "Is that okay with you?"

Garrett lifted an eyebrow but didn't address Aunt Shirley. He was staring at me. "We're having *plastic* flowers at our wedding?"

I gulped loudly. I knew there was no way he was going to believe anything I said.

"Of course not, you ninny." Aunt Shirley clucked her tongue and handed me another set of flowers. "You buy fake flowers and rearrange them to decide which flowers you want to carry in your bouquet."

Garrett's brow now furrowed. I could tell he was confused. It actually *did* sound like a plausible excuse. "So this has nothing to do with me coming down here to arrest Daniel? You didn't catch wind of this?"

My mouth dropped open. "You're arresting Daniel?"

"Hmm," Aunt Shirley said. "I didn't really see that one coming."

I wanted to ask about Ronni and all the money she'd suddenly come into, but I knew better. He'd never give me a straight answer.

"Stand back and let us do our job," Garrett said. "You can take pictures, but do it from afar."

"Sure thing, Ace," Aunt Shirley said.

Garrett shot her a dirty look and strode to the back of the store.

"Hey," Matt said as he followed behind Garrett, "don't forget we're having Sunday dinner for Father's Day over at Mom's this weekend."

"Believe me, I wouldn't miss it for the world." He had no idea the surprise he was in for.

"Well, you heard the man," Aunt Shirley said. "Pull out your phone and start snapping pics. Hank will kill us if we don't get something."

I quickly shoved the plastic flowers back in their spots then went to reach for my phone. Shouts and screams had me scrambling even faster in my pocket for my cell. No way was I missing this. Aunt Shirley was right, Hank would want pictures and reactions. I pulled up my camera app and we made our way to the back of the store where the shouts were coming from.

"You can't do this!" Daniel cried. "I didn't do anything!"

Blair and Lexi were huddled together in the doorframe as Daniel was being led out in handcuffs. His face was a dangerous shade of red.

I turned down the volume so no one would be able to hear the snapping of the pictures, then surreptitiously lifted my phone and started shooting. I didn't want to risk having Blair or Lexi see me. I still needed them to make my veil for the wedding.

"What exactly is he being charged with?" Blair asked as she wiped tears from her eyes.

Garrett passed a ranting Daniel off to Matt then turned to Blair and Lexi. "Money laundering, embezzlement, and tax evasion to start with. Then eventually murder, I'm sure."

"It wasn't me!" Daniel continued to shout as Matt led him away. "It was either Blair or Lexi. I don't know which, but it was one of them. I swear!"

Nothing like throwing your spouse under a bus!

Blair's knees buckled and Lexi did her best to help Blair stay upright.

"It's okay," Lexi said as she led Blair over to a chair. "He's delirious. He doesn't know what he's saying."

"Are you okay?" Garrett asked Blair.

"No, I'm not okay," Blair hissed. "What about my store? What will become of my store?"

"Ma'am, right now I'm focused on a murder investigation," Garrett replied briskly. "I have no idea what will become of your store."

Garrett turned and walked past me, his eyes never leaving my face. Once he passed, I turned around and watched his retreating backside. And what a lovely backside it was.

"Put your eyes back in your head," Aunt Shirley snickered, "and let's go see what we can find out."

I shoved my cell phone back into my pocket and went to stand by Blair and Lexi. Lexi was trying to calm down a hysterical Blair.

When Lexi saw us, her cheeks turned red. "Hello. I guess you heard all that?"

I gave her a sympathetic look. "Yes. I'm sorry."

Blair suddenly stood up. "Don't you worry. This will not put a crimp in your veil. We are on it."

"I know," I assured her. "There's plenty of time still."

Jeez! Your husband gets arrested for embezzling and murder and you're worried about a lace headband. Priceless!

"I can't believe it's Daniel they arrested," Aunt Shirley said. "That's too bad about him trying to place the blame on you, Blair."

Aunt Shirley...she's about as subtle as a volcanic explosion.

Blair narrowed her eyes. "I can assure you neither Lexi nor myself had anything to do with poor Samantha's death. Now, if you will excuse me, I need to call my divorce lawyer."

"Don't you mean criminal attorney?" Aunt Shirley asked.

"No."

Blair shoved past Lexi and slammed her office door shut. There are times when I wish the ground would just open up and swallow me.

"Don't worry about Blair," Lexi said. "She's been dealing with a lot lately."

So you keep saying.

"I'd like to stay and talk," Lexi said, "but the newsletters are due out today. I need to make sure everything looks good with emails."

"That's right," Aunt Shirley said. "We should be getting our notifications today about what's on sale this weekend."

Lexi winced. "Pretty much everything will be on sale and liquidated if things keep going as they are."

"Thanks for talking with us," I said. "We won't take up any more of your time."

Aunt Shirley and I hurried to the front of the store. Ronni and Willa were standing next to the register whispering back and forth with customers. Seeing as how she was so preoccupied, I didn't even raise my hand to wave to Willa.

"So is that it?" I asked as I headed the Falcon toward the newspaper office. "Do we even need to talk to Ronni and see how it is she's come up with all this money if the police have arrested Daniel?"

Aunt Shirley nodded. "You bet we do. Remember, Daniel is being arrested for embezzlement and tax evasion, not murder yet."

I had a sudden sinking feeling. This is usually where Aunt Shirley and I go and get ourselves in trouble. I sent up a silent prayer that Ronni would not be the murderer and try to kill us when we went to her place tonight.

CHAPTER 15

"Please tell me you two were at that frou frou store and you got pictures of whatever went down," Hank said by way of greeting when Aunt Shirley and I walked through the door of the *Granville Gazette.*

"Of course," Aunt Shirley said. "What do you take us for—amateurs?"

Hank raked his eyes over me and sneered…but said nothing. Good thing too, because I probably would have gone all spider monkey on him. Okay, maybe not. But it always sounds so good in my head.

"We got photos of Garrett hauling the owner's husband, Daniel Watkins, off for a number of charges," I said. "But technically I don't think one of those charges is murder."

Mindy looked up from her magazine. "What do you mean?"

I went over and sat down at my desk before answering. "Garrett named off a number of criminal charges, like embezzlement, money laundering, those types of crimes. It wasn't until later that he said the next logical thing would be for murder. So maybe they don't have enough just yet to arrest him for murder but they have proof of all the other charges."

Hank yanked out his unlit cigar. "I want an article and pics before you leave today. Understood?"

I heaved a sigh. Of course I knew that. He didn't have to tell me my job. "Understood."

Once Hank went back inside his office, I turned to Aunt Shirley. "I think we should just step back and let Garrett handle it from here."

"No way. Not gonna happen."

"What's going on?" Mindy asked.

I let out an exasperated sigh. "Aunt Shirley still wants to investigate. Before Daniel was arrested, we made an appointment tonight with Ronni. Aunt Shirley isn't convinced she's not the spy. We went by her house the other day and she's driving a new car and doing work on her house. The extra money has to be coming in from somewhere."

Mindy thought a moment. "So you think maybe Daniel is actually guilty of the embezzlement and money laundering, but not the murder?"

Aunt Shirley nodded her head vigorously. "Yep. I think the reason they can't arrest Daniel yet for murder is because they don't have any proof. This is just a fishing expedition today to see if he'll roll on himself for the murder."

Mindy looked pointedly at me. "And now Aunt Shirley thinks she knows who the murderer is and wants you two to go nab the killer tonight?"

I sighed again. "You know it."

Mindy took a sip of her herbal tea. "I don't like it. No offense, but you two seem to get yourselves in trouble a lot." Mindy turned to Aunt Shirley. "Maybe Ryli is correct on this one. Let Garrett handle it. Or at least give him your suspicions and let him take care of it."

Aunt Shirley narrowed her eyes at me. "Do you know how I got to be so good at my job as a private investigator?"

I closed my eyes and knew a lecture was coming. "No. How?"

"By being willing to take chances. By thinking outside the box. Do you seriously want to sit here and wait for someone else to grab your glory? Have I not taught you anything this year?"

It was on the tip of my tongue to tell her she taught me how to come inches within getting myself killed. But I couldn't hurt Aunt Shirley that way. I understood where she was coming from. I've grown up a lot this last year with her help. I just wished I wasn't constantly dealing with violence.

I smiled at her. "You've taught me how to read people better. You've taught me how to drive the Falcon like it's an extension of me. And you've taught me how to defend myself. So I guess we have no choice but to go to Ronni's house tonight and break her."

Aunt Shirley slapped her knee and laughed. "That's my girl!"

"Just promise me you'll be careful," Mindy said to me.

"I promise."

I activated my mouse and hunkered down at the keyboard. For the next few hours I worked diligently on writing an article for the paper about Daniel's arrest. I attached photos with the finished product and emailed it to Hank around lunchtime.

"The Manor is having a pretty good buffet lunch today," Aunt Shirley said. "I say we go there for lunch."

In all the time I'd known Aunt Shirley, I'd never known her to suggest eating at the cafeteria at the Manor. "Sure. What're they serving?"

"It's something new they're doing. Now that there's a weight room, swimming pool, and other health fitness rooms, the cafeteria jumped on board and started doing a buffet for lunch where you get a salad bar, couple choices of fish or other meats. They have a ton of different vegetables and soups to choose from." Aunt Shirley shrugged. "It's actually really good. I eat for free, but you'll have to pay like five bucks. You can't beat that."

I grabbed my purse. "Sounds good. I'm starving." I turned to Mindy. "Do you want anything while we're out?"

"No, thanks. I'm going to head home early today. I want to make a nice dinner for Hank tonight. You girls go have fun. And please be careful tonight at Ronni's house."

With a promise we would, Aunt Shirley and I piled into the Falcon and headed to the visitor's parking at Oak Grove Manor. I was glad Aunt Shirley was embracing the Manor life. For the longest time she refused to try and make friends, she didn't decorate her apartment because she swore she was only staying for a few months, and she refused to participate in any activities the Manor provided.

I found a parking spot and strode inside the Manor behind Aunt Shirley. We made a beeline straight for the cafeteria. As we stood in line, I dug in my purse for money. The smells coming from the room were exquisite.

"It smells wonderful," I said.

"It is!" I turned and saw Old Man Jenkins making his way slowly toward us. "I eat here every day now. Don't I?" He looked at Aunt Shirley for confirmation, but she was suddenly interested in watching people pile food on their plates.

Could Aunt Shirley have suggested this place because she knew Old Man Jenkins eats here every day?

I nudged Aunt Shirley and gave her a wicked grin. "Old Man Jenkins says he eats here every day. Did you know that?"

"How would I know that?" Aunt Shirley snapped. But I could see the start of a blush on her cheeks "It's not like I pay attention to his eating habits."

Oh, I think you do!

"Will you eat lunch with us, Mr. Jenkins?"

Mr. Jenkins's face lit up. "I'd be honored to eat with the two most beautiful women in the room."

"Hear that, Aunt Shirley? He thinks we're the most beautiful women in the room."

"Well, the fool has cataracts," Aunt Shirley grumbled under her breath.

When it was my turn to pay the cashier, I gave her my money and followed Aunt Shirley to the buffet line. I grabbed a plate and started building a salad.

Aunt Shirley leaned in toward me. "Why'd you go and do a gol-durned fool thing like that for? I didn't want to eat lunch with him!"

I looked over and saw Old Man Jenkins shuffling his way to the buffet...his grin nearly split his face in two. "Well, I do. You're free to eat wherever you want."

Aunt Shirley narrowed her eyes at me. "Don't try and one-up me, girl. I know what you're doing here."

Any other time I would back down and cower to Aunt Shirley. But I realized she was right. I had grown up a lot this last year. I no longer wanted to be the meek, mild girl wondering through life. If life pushed me...I was going to push back!

I sprinkled some sunflower seeds on the top of my salad and grabbed a vinaigrette. "Like I said, I want to sit with him. You're free to do whatever you want."

126

Aunt Shirley growled but made no further comment. Ryli one…Aunt Shirley zero.

I decided to start with a salad and go back later for the meat and potatoes part of the meal. I walked over to an empty table that sat four people. A pitcher of water was already sitting on the table.

"So how's the investigation going?" Old Man Jenkins asked once we'd eaten a few bites of our meal.

"Pretty good, actually." I took a sip of water. "The police have arrested someone, but Aunt Shirley and I are going out tonight to interview someone else we think might be involved."

Old Man Jenkins' face showed concern. "You girls be careful. If you need any help, you just call on me."

Aunt Shirley huffed. "The day I need help from an old man like you will be the day I roll over and get married."

I sucked in my breath at Aunt Shirley's rudeness.

I looked over at Old Man Jenkins. Instead of looking insulted, he looked amused. He lifted a brow on his saggy, wrinkled face. "Then I'll be holding you to that promise, Shirley Andrews."

My mouth dropped open. I mentally high-fived Old Man Jenkins for successfully backing Aunt Shirley into a corner. Looks like Old Man Jenkins was here to stay and he was ready to fight.

"You're an old fool, Waylon Jenkins." But I could tell by the look on Aunt Shirley's face that she was shaken. "I need some more food." She got up from the table and practically sprinted to the buffet line.

I looked back at Old Man Jenkins, but he was calmly eating his soup. He caught my stare and winked at me.

Game…set…match!

"Waylon, huh?" I asked for lack of anything better to say.

"Yep. Family name."

The rest of the lunch was eaten in silence. When we were through, Old Man Jenkins stood up. "Thank you, ladies, for having lunch with me. I enjoyed it immensely. Now, if you will excuse me, I hear a checkers game calling me." He bowed to us both and left.

"Don't say anything!" Aunt Shirley hissed. "The nerve of that man thinking I was proposing to him!"

I hid my smile behind my water glass and said nothing.

Without a care in the world, Aunt Shirley reached up and yanked out her top teeth. "Got me a pepper stuck up here and it hurts."

I winced and wondered if Old Man Jenkins knew what he was in for.

CHAPTER 16

"I brought my nunchucks just in case." Aunt Shirley slid into the Falcon and patted her huge pink purse.

After lunch Aunt Shirley and I decided to stay at the Manor and practice kicking a weapon out of an assailant's hand. Since that was the next move I was going to demonstrate to the class, I figured I better learn it beforehand.

Aunt Shirley showed me how to lean sideways to help with momentum and to get my leg higher in the air so I could make contact with the bad guy's hand. By the tenth attempt, I finally had it down.

I'd then left Aunt Shirley at the Manor and headed back to the office and answered phones since Mindy was gone. I left the office around five and came straight to the Manor to pick up Aunt Shirley.

"You won't need them," I said firmly. Aunt Shirley was constantly hurting herself more than the bad guy every time she tried to use them.

"Never know," she countered.

I squelched a sigh and proceeded toward Ronni's house.

"I texted Garrett and told him we were going to Ronni's house for a while."

Aunt Shirley scowled and opened her mouth.

I cut her off. "Don't worry. I didn't tell him our suspicions. I told him she was upset and wanted to talk. But I didn't want to go in there blind. If it turns out she's the killer, someone needs to know where we are."

Aunt Shirley stared at me. "If it turns out she's the killer, we're taking her down!"

"We're a little early," I said. "How about we run through the drive-thru and get something to drink."

"Fine. And speaking of drinks, once this case is solved, I'm ready to toss back a few tequila shots. I haven't had time to let my hair down and boogie lately."

I barely refrained from mentioning to her that her short, multi-colored hair couldn't be let down, and that no one boogies anymore.

We pulled into Ronni's driveway just as she was stepping out of her sports car. "Good timing," she said. "C'mon in and I'll make us some coffee. I baked a coffee cake yesterday, so it should still be good."

We followed her into the house.

"Careful. I'm doing some remodeling, so it's a little messy. There might be nails or screws on the floor."

I glanced at Aunt Shirley. She was giving me a knowing look.

Aunt Shirley and I sat down at the kitchen table as Ronni prepared coffee and sliced us each a big piece of coffee cake. She set creamer and sugar on the table and poured three glasses of coffee.

"This is really good," I said as I swallowed my first bite of the coffee cake.

"Thanks," Ronni said. "It was my mom's recipe."

There was an awkward pause.

"So, what exactly did you want to talk with me about?" Ronni asked. "The craziness that's been going on down at the store?"

"Yes," Aunt Shirley confirmed. "Just some questions about what's going on at the store."

Ronni crinkled her nose. "I hope you don't mind, but I don't want to say anything bad about what's going on."

"Of course," I assured her. "It's more about your observations."

"Speaking of observations," Aunt Shirley said. "You've mentioned you're remodeling the house, and I couldn't help but notice your fancy car in the drive. I'm wondering how you've managed to acquire these things on a cashier's salary."

Ronni's face turned red. "Wait. Are you accusing me of something?"

"Not at all," I said quickly. "It's just an observation."

Ronni shoved back her coffee cake. "I'd rather not talk about where the money is coming from, if you don't mind."

I actually do mind. I'm beginning to lean more toward not only are you the spy...but you're the murderer!

"Of course, dear," Aunt Shirley soothed. "Now, about the store. Have you noticed anyone acting suspicious lately? Acting in a way they typically wouldn't? Buying things they usually couldn't afford?"

Ronni's nostrils flared. "I think I get where you're going. But let me say you're on the wrong track."

I was hoping Aunt Shirley had a firm grasp on her nunchucks, because something told me the poop was about to hit the fan!

"When we put everything together," Aunt Shirley continued, "you're the only person we couldn't figure out. Where did this sudden increase of income come from? It's common knowledge that someone has been leaking information to a rival company. And usually the person that leaks the information gets compensation in the form of lots of money."

Ronni's lips pinched together. She turned to look at me. "Because I know your mom, I'm going to try and remind myself that you're just trying to help. But you are way off."

My heart dropped a little. It always made me feel guilty when people mentioned my mom. Like somehow she raised a bad daughter, but they were willing to overlook it because Mom was so awesome.

"Then why don't you enlighten us?" Aunt Shirley said. She reached inside her purse, took out her nunchucks, and set them on the table.

Ronni's eyes doubled in size. "What are you doing?"

"Nothing," Aunt Shirley said. "Just thought I'd clean out my purse while you talked."

I bit my tongue to keep from snickering.

"Fine," Ronni huffed. "I didn't want to make it public, but I'll tell you what I've been doing for extra money." Without another word she got up and left the table.

Was she going to get a gun?

"Should we be panicking right now?" I asked.

Aunt Shirley furrowed her brow. "I'm not sure."

A few minutes later Ronni came back in carrying quilts and various other items. She laid them on the table. "I've been selling crafts on Etsy. I made quilts from scraps at the store. And before you ask, Blair knows I take the scraps. She lets me have them for free."

My heart fell a little lower in my stomach. We'd made a huge mistake.

"I also make Christmas tree ornaments, hot pads, rugs, everything out of scraps. I make a pretty darn good living doing these things. So before you go accusing me of something that isn't true, maybe you need to think about your next move."

Oh, crap!

I tried to backpedal as much as I could, but I knew we were totally in the wrong. "I'm sorry, Ronni. We were wrong in assuming you'd do anything illegal just for the sake of a few dollars."

"Technically, corporate espionage is more than a few dollars," Aunt Shirley corrected me.

I glared at her.

Aunt Shirley shrugged. "I'm just saying."

"Please accept our apologies," I said. "We just wanted to make sure, for Samantha's sake, that her killer was brought to justice."

Ronni ran her hand down one of the quilts. "I do understand. I want the same thing. I really liked Samantha, and I'm having a hard time with what's happened. I'm also terrified the store will close, and not only will I lose my job, but I'll lose the income from my side business, too."

"Can you forgive us?" I asked as Aunt Shirley shoved her nunchucks back inside her purse.

"Yes," Ronni said softly. "Besides, I thought they caught Samantha's killer when they arrested Daniel this morning. We were told by Blair this morning that Daniel has been stealing money from the company and changing the reports. Samantha found out, confronted him, and that's why he killed her."

"Blair told you guys that?" I asked.

"Yes. After the police left, she closed the shop for an hour and called an emergency store meeting."

Interesting.

"But I can't help but think we're missing something," I said.

Aunt Shirley nodded. "Me, too."

"I'm sorry I can't help," Ronni said. "I haven't seen or heard of anyone coming into money lately. Well, except for Daniel, of course."

"Thanks for your time," I said as Ronni led us to her door. "And don't worry, your secret is safe with us. If you don't want people knowing you have a second job, we won't tell anyone."

"Thanks."

She stood in the doorway and lifted her hand as we drove away.

"Well, that was anticlimactic," I grumbled. "I guess maybe Ronni is right. The only person that's recently come into a lot of money is Daniel. Maybe it's from both selling information to a rival company and from embezzling from the company."

Aunt Shirley shrugged, her face dejected. "I guess it could be true."

We were silent as I drove the rest of the way to the Manor. Aunt Shirley gathered her purse and opened the door.

"I'm going to text Garrett in a while and see how his interrogation is going," I said.

Aunt Shirley smiled. "And I'm going to go drink a toast to a killer being apprehended."

I laughed. "Have fun!"

CHAPTER 17

"Hey, Miss Molly." I leaned down and scooped the cat up in my arms as I shuffled toward the kitchen. I got down a can of her favorite cat food and shook it into her pink-studded bowl.

"We're having a celebratory dinner tonight," I informed her. "Looks like Garrett has gotten his killer."

Miss Molly meowed and sprang from my arms. I set the bowl down on the kitchen floor and walked to my bedroom. It was a long day and I was tired. I wanted nothing more than to strip and crawl into bed.

I'd just slipped off my shoes when my cell rang with a notification. I figured Garrett was thinking of me as I was thinking of him. I swiped at the phone and realized it was the auto-generated email from Quilter's Paradise. I was in the process of deleting the email when another text came through.

I pulled it up and realized it was also the auto-generated text from Quilter's Paradise. I groaned and realized I must have accidentally signed up for both email and text for ways to receive weekly information. I was about to delete the text when I noticed it wasn't what I thought it was.

It was a text asking me to come to the store. There was a problem with the wedding veil that needed my immediate attention. I was to park in the back and come to the fitting room I was in for my previous fitting.

I suddenly went on alert. My phone said it was six-thirty. It was well past the time for Quilter's Paradise to be closed. Who would still be at the shop working? Blair? Lexi? Willa if she had a key? Could Ronni have driven back to the store quickly to send this message?

I could feel my heart beating wildly in my chest. I wasn't sure what to do. Did I call Aunt Shirley and take her with me? What if there really was a problem with the veil and that was all it was. How silly would I look if I brought backup?

I sent a quick text to Aunt Shirley asking her what she was doing.

A few seconds later I got her reply. She was already three tequila shots in to having a good night.

So much for bringing Aunt Shirley with me.

I sent her a text to have fun and let her know I had to go to Quilter's Paradise for a veil fix.

I quickly changed into a pair of yoga pants, t-shirt, and flip flops. I grabbed my purse and headed out the door. As I drove to Quilter's Paradise, I willed my heart to stop racing.

I parked in the back like requested, then yanked the store's door open. It was pitch black except for a soft fluorescent glow coming from one of the rooms down the hall.

"Hello? Blair? Lexi? Anyone here?"

"Back here," Blair called.

I took a deep breath and slowly let it out. I could do this. I'd been learning for almost a year now under Aunt Shirley, and I knew some self-defense moves. If I had to, I could fight my way out.

I was about to step into the room when my cell vibrated. I pulled up a text message from Aunt Shirley.

"I know who the killer is! Do not go to Quilter's Paradise! I repeat, do not go! I'm on my way just in case you don't get this!"

What the heck?

I was about to turn around and run back out of the store when Lexi stepped in the hallway—gun in hand.

"Ryli! So glad you made it. Come in. We're about ready to get this party started."

Lexi grabbed me by my arm and shoved me into the room. I saw Blair tied to a chair. She had tears running down her face.

I swallowed hard. "What's going on, Lexi?"

Lexi sneered at me. "Like you don't know. I'm just surprised that meddlesome aunt isn't with you."

Never have I been so thankful that I didn't have Aunt Shirley tag along. Of course, she said she was on her way so she could be in danger soon. I couldn't help but wonder how Aunt Shirley planned on getting here since I was her ride.

"Lexi, why are you doing this?" Blair whined.

Lexi pushed against my back and I stumbled over my feet and landed hard on my knees.

"Like you don't know!" Lexi yelled. "Get up, Ryli, and sit on the couch."

I scrambled up and sat on the couch. Lexi paced back and forth in front of us. I could tell she was ready to explode.

"I can't believe you were stupid enough to come tonight," Lexi snorted.

"I didn't realize you were the killer," I countered back. "Why did you kill Samantha?"

"That idiot thought she figured it all out. She did the one thing no one else could…not even that boyfriend of yours, Ryli. He has Daniel holed up on embezzlement charges, hoping for a murder conviction."

"For those of us getting in the game late," I said, "why don't you start from the beginning." I was hoping to stall until Aunt Shirley arrived.

"Have you ever asked yourself why this company isn't mine?" Lexi demanded. She walked over to the desk in the room and took out a pair of scissors. She opened the blades up and held one side like a knife.

The spit in my mouth dried up.

"No, not really," I said. "I figured it's not yours because Blair and her husband started it."

Lexi let out a barking laugh. "Because I didn't have the startup money. This whole thing was my idea! I was the one that put the thought into Blair's head. The only thing I lacked was funds."

"That's not true!" Blair cried. "I didn't even know you until I hired you!"

Lexi walked over and swiped the scissor blade across Blair's forearm.

Blair screamed in pain.

I clamped my hands over my mouth to keep from screaming, also.

"It *is* true! I'm the person that brought this company to where it is! I was the one that told you about the value of internet advertising. I was the one that had the business degree. You only had money to start the company. This company should be mine!

I'm the one with the vision! Instead, I barely make a living working as your slave!"

I could tell Blair wanted to argue, but she was terrified of what Lexi would do next.

Lexi turned to me, twirling the scissors in front of her face. Blood ran down one of the blades. "I tried at first to be Blair's friend. To try and bond with her over the company, this way she might give me a bigger piece of the pie. But she's so selfish. She only used me for my ideas and turned my friendship away."

"No!" Blair cried. "You have always been a—"

"Lying bitch!" Lexi slashed out again, this time making contact with Blair's cheek.

Blair let out a scream that had my insides turning cold. I knew without a doubt I couldn't talk Lexi off this ledge. She was ready to torture. She was ready to kill.

"So I bid my time," Lexi said as she leaned down and wiped the blood lovingly off Blair's cheek. "I played the dutiful co-worker." Lexi caressed Blair's cheek. "Why, I even befriended you husband. He was much easier to manipulate and get what I wanted."

Blair turned her head away and let the tears fall.

"And you never knew!" Lexi laughed cruelly. "One night when Daniel was all alone, yet again, I struck." Lexi turned to me. "Blair was so dedicated to seeing her store in Columbia succeed that she didn't realize she was neglecting her husband."

"No!" Blair whispered. "You slept with my husband?"

Lexi grinned maliciously at Blair. "On more than one occasion. It was a pattern. I'd get him drunk, plant a seed in his head about how wonderful he was and how you were taking advantage of him. How he could probably steal you blind and you'd never know because you paid that little attention to him."

Lexi reached out and grabbed Blair's chin. "I was the one that convinced him to embezzle and bankrupt you."

"You've worked for this company for years. How could you?"

Lexi leaned down within an inch of Blair's face. "Easily. And while he was crippling you financially, I was meeting with your competitors and selling them information. I also went about crippling this store's reputation by logging on to different computers at various locations and writing bad reviews."

Is this what Aunt Shirley meant when she said she figured it out? How?

"I thought you told me you were home the night Samantha was killed," I said.

Lexi gave me a pitying look. "I lied. It's what I do." Her eyes suddenly darkened. "And don't think I'm not going to take my sweet time with you. *You* are the reason this whole thing has gone bad! My intent was to set up Daniel, crush Blair emotionally and financially, and then swoop in and save the day by buying her out. But then *you* had to go and ruin it! I have no idea what will happen to the shop now. I'm going to have to start all over from scratch. And for that reason, you're gonna die slowly!"

I had to force myself to continue breathing. The fear was that real.

"Why did you kill Samantha?" I asked again.

"Like I said, she *thought* she'd figured it out. Of course, I had no idea that she had went blabbing to you and your aunt. But after everyone had gone home that night, she called me and asked me to meet her at the store. She had proof that Daniel was not only giving information to the competition in Kansas City, but that he was stealing from the store. So I drove back into Granville and parked in the back. I found her going over Daniel's ledgers and spreadsheets. See, she had no idea that Daniel wasn't really behind all the embezzling...I was. She told me she thought that Daniel was selling information to the rival stores and that he was taking money from the store. She told me about you and your aunt coming in the morning and having the back door unlocked for you. I listened to her, pretended to be sympathetic where I should be. Then when the time was right, I reached over and grabbed the cutting shears and gave chase to her. You should have seen the shocked look on her face. Like she was trying to put it all together as she was running for her life. I couldn't have planned it any better when I realized she still had a firm grasp on one of Daniel's ledgers. It was perfect for framing Daniel."

Lexi had completely lost it. I knew my time to strike was now or never. Lexi had finished telling her story. She wouldn't think twice about killing us off now.

I thought back to all the things I'd learned in my self-defense class. How to yell at your assailant and take them by surprise. How to grab hold of a bad guy. I'd even just practiced how to kick a weapon out of an assailant's hand today. I stood up from the couch.

"Sit down!" Lexi demanded as she turned to me. "I'll get to you in a minute. I just wish your aunt was here so I could cut her up, too."

"NO!" I screamed.

Lexi reared back, shocked. "I said sit down!"

"NO!" I screamed again. This time I reached for the scissors. Unfortunately, I wasn't looking at her, I was looking at the weapon. With my concentration on carefully grabbing the weapon, I didn't realize I left my face vulnerable. With her left hand, Lexi reached up and socked me in the eye.

I fell back onto the couch.

Blinking around the stars I was seeing, I stood up again.

"You are a glutton for punishment, aren't you?" Lexi laughed.

She held up the scissors like she was going to stab me. I leaned sideways and kicked with my foot. My flip flop flew through the air and my bare foot made contact.

"Ouch!" Lexi screamed. "What the hell are you doing? You kicked me in my boob!"

I set my foot down and looked at Lexi. She was still in shock over my ineptness. I decided to strike again while the iron was hot and I went to flip her over my shoulder.

I pivoted with my back to her, holding the scissors out in front of my body so she couldn't stab me, and pushed my butt into her stomach.

She didn't budge.

"Are you trying to flip me over?" Lexi asked incredulously. "What kind of self-defense class did you take? A how-to-annoy-your-attacker-into-killing-you class?"

She stepped back from my protruding butt and kicked me swiftly with her foot. I flew forward and fell on my hands and knees. Pain radiated throughout my body and my palms started to tingle.

This was going to be a lot harder than I thought.

I scrambled to my feet and turned around. Aunt Shirley and Old Man Jenkins were standing in the doorway, each with shocked looks on their faces. I groaned. They must have seen me getting my butt kicked.

Aunt Shirley recovered quickly. "You want us, Lexi. Come get us!"

Aunt Shirley grabbed Old Man Jenkins by the arm and together they ran down the hall and out into the store. In a fit of rage, Lexi ran after them. I kicked off my other flip flop and scrambled after Lexi, ignoring the cries from Blair to untie her.

I ran out of the hallway and into the store. Aunt Shirley and Old Man Jenkins pivoted and were now facing Lexi. She stopped and looked at them. Then Lexi turned to look at me. She knew she was outnumbered. She'd left the gun on the desk and all she had was scissors.

I took a step forward and was about to close her in when the back door to the store burst open.

"Police!" Garrett cried. "Lexi Miller, get down on the ground and put your hands behind your back!"

Lexi whirled around and saw Garrett, Matt, and I coming toward her. She turned back around and thought she had a better chance with Aunt Shirley and Old Man Jenkins. Aunt Shirley must have sensed it, too.

Aunt Shirley took one step toward her, hunched down, and wiggled her hands. "C'mon, girl. You think you can take me? Let's go!"

With a warrior-like scream, Lexi raised her scissors in the air and ran full tilt at Aunt Shirley. Aunt Shirley was rocking side to side, squatting at her hips.

144

Before Lexi had an opportunity to strike at Aunt Shirley, Old Man Jenkins took a huge step forward and punched Lexi in the throat with his fist.

She instantly dropped to the ground, clutched her throat, rolling and moaning in pain.

"What the hell was that?" Aunt Shirley exclaimed as Garrett ran over to Lexi, flipped her over, handcuffed her, and hauled her up. "I had her!"

Old Man Jenkins smiled slyly. "I had her, too."

Aunt Shirley narrowed her eyes at him. "Where did you learn that move?"

Mr. Jenkins lifted a brow at Aunt Shirley's tone of voice. "Not that you ever asked, Shirley Andrews, but I did serve in the Korean War. I am military trained."

Aunt Shirley's mouth dropped. "You're former military? Why didn't you ever tell me?"

Old Man Jenkins shrugged. "Didn't see a point to." He grinned wickedly at Aunt Shirley. "Besides, I figured you're already indebted to me because you had to ask me for help to get over here. And we all know that today at lunch you said the day you had to ask me for help would be the day you marry me. I figured the least I could do was defend your honor and take down the killer."

Aunt Shirley looked like she'd swallowed a huge bag of lemons.

I snickered. *Looks like your big mouth finally got you in trouble!*

CHAPTER 18

"How did you know Lexi was the killer?" I asked Aunt Shirley once Matt had taken Lexi down to the station and Officer Ryan had untied Blair.

Aunt Shirley was still visibly shaken by the comment Old Man Jenkins had previously made.

"Yes," Garrett said. "How did you know?"

Aunt Shirley pulled out her phone and pulled up her newsletter from the store. "I don't know what made me read the newsletter. But the first thing I saw was the affirmation at the top of the page. It says, 'You Are Radiant and Noble.' And something just clicked."

"What?" Garrett and I asked at the same time.

"Put the first letter of each word together...what do you have?"

"Yarn!" I exclaimed. "Lexi was using a code and dropping clues to the competing company in the weekly newsletter. Great job, Aunt Shirley!"

Aunt Shirley preened. "All in a day's work."

"How did you know to be here?" I asked Garrett.

"I texted him," Aunt Shirley said. "When I realized who the killer was, I was afraid I couldn't reach you in time, so I texted Garrett and told him to get to the quilt store immediately. You were in trouble."

146

"Your eye looks nasty," Garrett said. "Did the paramedics look at it?"

"Yes. Not much they can do for a black eye."

Garrett grinned at me. "It's kinda sexy."

I wrapped my arms around Garrett. "Thanks for coming."

He kissed me on my forehead. "I can't believe I'm going to say this, but it's Aunt Shirley you need to thank. Daniel had just admitted that he was having an affair with Lexi, so I decided to take a break from the interrogation. It's pure luck that I read the text message within ten minutes after Aunt Shirley sent it. Before that, we hadn't taken a break in hours."

"Oh, now." Aunt Shirley waved her hand dismissively at me. "I'm just glad Old Man Jenkins was playing checkers when I ran down to see who was available in the great room to drive me somewhere."

Old Man Jenkins smiled at me. "Did my heart good to hear her ask me for help. Does this mean you're gonna be the Maid of Honor at the wedding?"

Garrett's mouth dropped. "What wedding?"

"Hush your mouth," Aunt Shirley snapped. "There ain't gonna be no dang wedding! I ain't marrying you, you old fool!"

Old Man Jenkins winked at me. "We'll see."

***

Blair Watkins called me the next morning and asked if Aunt Shirley and I would come in to the store. She had something to tell us. I almost didn't come. It was Saturday and I needed to rest. Besides, my eye hurt much worse the next day.

I did what I could to cover the black eye, threw on some clothes, then went to pick Aunt Shirley up from the Manor. We were at Quilter's Paradise by nine o'clock.

"Thanks for all your help," Blair said as we sat on her couch in her office. "I don't know what would have happened to me if you guys hadn't been there to take Lexi down."

"It was nothing," Aunt Shirley said modestly. "All in a day's work for us. Right, Ryli?"

I chuckled. "Right."

"Well, to show my appreciation, I want you to know that I'm going to make your wedding veil for free. I figure it's the least I can do. Now that I know Daniel was cooking the books and Lexi is behind bars getting ready to be arraigned on murder charges, I feel I am able to take back my life. So as a thank you I want to make your veil for you."

Tears filled my eyes. "Thank you. I'd love that."

Aunt Shirley and I left the store and went to the newspaper office. I knew Hank would be pacing and cursing by the time I walked in.

I wasn't disappointed.

"Where the hell have you been? I have a deadline for printing in one hour! I need a story!"

"Cool your jets," I said. "I wrote something last night and will submit it within the half hour."

Hank visibly relaxed...then looked me over. "You look like you got the crap kicked out of you."

Aunt Shirley snickered. "You're gonna need to help her on those self-defense moves. She's really bad."

148

I stuck my tongue out at Aunt Shirley, ignored Hank's laughter, and booted up my computer. I ran through the story one more time, then sent the story to Hank.

It was only ten and I wanted to go home and rest.

"Why don't you take the rest of the day off," Mindy suggested. "You look like you're about ready to fall on your face."

"Sounds good to me," Aunt Shirley said. "I could use a little more sleep."

"What exactly have you done to warrant sleep?" I asked snidely.

"I solved this murder!"

Mindy chuckled at us, then shooed us out the door. "I'll see you guys tomorrow at your mom's house for the big Father's Day dinner."

I groaned. I'd completely forgotten. I turned to Aunt Shirley. "We need to go by Mom's and see what she needs us to do for the dinner."

I didn't really want to see Mom while sporting a black eye. I knew she was going to freak. But I had no choice. I drove us over to Mom's to see what was going on. Her and Paige were in the kitchen pouring over recipes.

"I can't believe your face," Mom said as she shook her head sadly at me.

I laughed self-consciously and tentatively touched my eye. "It doesn't hurt as much today."

Liar!

"I can't believe Lexi was the killer," Paige said. She set a glass of iced tea in front of me before sitting at the table beside me.

"Aunt Shirley and I came to see what we can do for tomorrow's dinner," I said, hoping to change the subject.

Paige did a little wiggle dance in her chair. "I'm so excited! This will definitely be a Father's Day your brother won't forget!"

CHAPTER 19

"The meal looks lovely, Janine," Paige's dad said as he plopped a heaping spoonful of mashed potatoes on his plate. "Thank you for inviting us today."

Mom smiled surreptitiously at Paige. "My pleasure."

I glanced around the table. Mom, Doc, Paige, Matt, Garrett, Paige's parents, Aunt Shirley, and even Hank and Mindy were in attendance. Only a handful of us knew what was about to happen.

"Here," Paige said as she handed Matt two pieces of chicken.

He laughed. "I don't think I need two."

Paige gave him a brilliant smile. "You want two, trust me. You need to keep up your strength."

Matt had just started eating when I jumped up out of my chair. "Oh, I forgot something in the kitchen." I ran into the kitchen, grabbed my clue, and came back to the table and handed Matt a single pea.

"Um, thanks."

I laughed at his expression. "Open up the pea."

Matt looked warily at me as he popped opened the pea.

"How many little peas are there inside the pod?" I asked.

"Two."

I gave him a huge smile. "Oh, good. That's what I was hoping for."

I laughed gleefully at his confused look.

"I forgot something," Mom said suddenly. She got up, went into the kitchen, and came back out carrying two bottles of beer. She set them down in front of Matt.

He frowned up at Mom. "What's going on? I don't need two beers. Heck, I don't need one beer."

I chuckled. "Trust me. You do."

He shot a confused look to Paige. She ignored him and continued eating. Garrett was giving me a confused look as well. I smiled and went back to eating.

The conversation was pleasant and the meal was great...but it couldn't end fast enough for me. I was anxious to give Matt his next set of clues.

"Dessert!" Mom cried cheerfully as she dashed into the kitchen.

"What's going on with you guys?" Garrett hissed in my ear. "You ladies are acting funny."

I gave him my best blank stare.

It wasn't good enough because he lifted one brow at me.

I was saved from having to answer when Mom came back in the room carrying two trays of cupcakes.

"I couldn't make up my mind," Mom said. "So I thought I'd make two different kinds." She placed two cupcakes on Matt's dirty dinner plate.

He looked up at Mom. "Okay. Something's going on. What gives?"

She kissed him on the brow. "It's your first Father's Day. Paige, Ryli, and I just wanted to make it spectacular."

Mom passed the rest of the trays around and we all took cupcakes.

"Hey," Hank said. "Why's mine got pink on the inside and Mindy's got blue?"

Time to strike!

"Paige," I said. "Aren't you hot in that sweater?"

"I am, Ryli. Thank you for asking."

Paige stood up, unbuttoned her sweater, and flung it off her body. Her t-shirt read, "I don't always make a baby...but when I do, I make sure to make two!"

A collective gasp went up at the dinner table.

I swear you could hear a pin drop.

Then chaos!

"What's going on?"

"Does this mean what I think it means?"

"Twins!"

I looked over at Matt's face. I could tell his brain wasn't allowing him to process everything.

"Maybe this will help." I reached under my dinner plate and took out an envelope. I had been entrusted with the sonogram picture because Paige did not want to know the sex of the babies beforehand.

I handed Matt the envelope.

He reached out and took it...his hands shaking.

He ripped it open and sat in stunned silence. Tears fell from his eyes. He looked at me. "I don't know whether to laugh at what you've done to my children, or ban you from ever babysitting."

I knew Paige didn't want to know the sex, so I made a copy of the original and glued little tiny neon green light sabers to where the sex would be. This way no one but me knew what was coming down the pike for Paige and Matt.

Paige leaned over and looked at the sonogram and laughed. "Thank you for hiding the sex."

"I can't believe this," Matt said quietly. He turned to Paige. "I'm having twins?"

She laughed. "Well, technically *I'm* having twins. You just fathered them!"

With a jubilant cry, Matt hugged Paige. Both of them weeping with joy.

Soon, there wasn't a dry eye at the table...even crusty Hank was sniffing and gulping down water. Paige's parents jumped up and hugged everyone, both of them crying. Mom and Paige's mom started talking baby names, and Mindy was already planning a baby shower.

I sat quietly and watched as everyone cried, made future plans for the babies, and patted each other on the back as though *they* all had just made two babies. This was definitely a Father's Day to remember.

Garrett reached over and clasped my hand. "I'm happy for them. But I can't wait for this to be us."

I shivered. For the first time in a long time, I felt at peace about my future with Garrett. Most days I'm worried I won't be able to be what he wants in a wife. I don't cook, I don't clean house very well, I don't listen to what he tells me. But then I realized...that's my fear. Not his. He's never once asked me or expected me to be a chef, a housewife, a stay-at-home mom. All he's ever asked me to be is myself.

Aunt Shirley cackled and all eyes turned to her. "Before you go wishing for babies of your own, Garrett. Just remember we have one more important event."

154

Garrett's ears turned pink. "I'm aware we need to get married still."

Aunt Shirley waved her hand in the air. "Heck no. I ain't talking about the wedding. I'm talking about the bachelorette party!"

I groaned loudly. I remember what happened at the last bachelorette party we had. No way was I repeating something like that.

"I'm thinking Vegas!" Aunt Shirley shouted.

ABOUT THE AUTHOR

Jenna writes in the genre of cozy/women's literature. Her humorous characters and stories revolve around over-the-top family members, creative murders, and there's always a positive element of the military in her stories. Jenna currently lives in Missouri with her fiancé, step-daughter, Nova Scotia duck tolling retriever dog, Brownie, and her tuxedo-cat, Whiskey. She is a former court reporter turned educator turned full-time writer. She has a Master's degree in Special Education, and an Education Specialist degree in Curriculum and Instruction. She also spent twelve years in full-time ministry.

When she's not writing, Jenna likes to attend beer and wine tastings, go antiquing, visit craft festivals, and spend time with her family and friends. You can friend request her on Facebook under Jenna St. James, and she has a blog http://jennastjames.blogspot.com/. You can also e-mail her at authorjennastjames@gmail.com.

Jenna writes both the Ryli Sinclair Mystery and the Sullivan Sisters Mystery. You can purchase these books at http://amazon.com/author/jennastjames. Thank you for taking the time to read Jenna St. James' books. If you enjoy her books, please leave a review on Amazon, Goodreads, or any other social media outlet.

Made in the USA
Columbia, SC
25 August 2018